COMHAIRLE CHONTAE ROSCOMÁIN
LEABHARLANNA CHONTAE ROSCOMÁIN

6363727   F

1. This book may be retained for three weeks.
2. This book may be renewed if not requested by another borrower.

About the Author

After modern literature studies at the Sorbonne, Caroline Caugant decided to become a writer, alongside her work as a graphic designer. She lives in Paris.

CAROLINE CAUGANT

Sunlight Hours

Translated from French by Jackie Smith

HODDER &
STOUGHTON

First published in France in 2019 by Editions Stock
An Hachette France company, under the title *Les Heures Solaires*

First published in Great Britain in 2020 by Hodder & Stoughton
An Hachette UK company

I

A CIP catalogue record for this title
is available from the British Library

Trade Paperback ISBN 978 1 529 34229 1
eBook ISBN 978 1 529 34230 7

Typeset in Plantin Light by Palimpsest Book Production Limited,
Falkirk, Stirlingshire

Printed and bound in Great Britain by Clays Ltd, Elcograf S.p.A.

Hodder & Stoughton policy is to use papers that are natural, renewable
and recyclable products and made from wood grown in sustainable
forests. The logging and manufacturing processes are expected to
conform to the environmental regulations of the country of origin.

Hodder & Stoughton Ltd
Carmelite House
50 Victoria Embankment
London EC4Y 0DZ

www.hodder.co.uk

If one doesn't talk about a thing, it has never happened.
It is simply expression that gives reality to things.

OSCAR WILDE

Contents

Prologue

It's a clear night. Not the kind of night Louise would have chosen for her final farewell. She would have preferred it stormy. Going out with a bang.

A breeze steals into the flat through the half-open window, carrying with it the scent of chrysanthemums. Fingers trace the outline of a head, thinning hair, a broken neck. The lines of the face emerge little by little to the rasp of charcoal on canvas. Then comes the body, the protruding belly, supple as rubber. As the city sleeps, the figure frees itself from the canvas. A thinker with jet-black eyes, piercing as a cat's, comes to life.

Lured by the light fixed above the easel, a mosquito circles around in its halo. Even gorged with blood, it is minute compared to the big water mosquitoes that used to dance above the flat expanses of the river in V. Billie watches the insect for a moment before crushing it with a sharp blow. The blood mingles with the charcoal powder on her skin.

She stands up and goes to open the other living room window to create a draught. Down below, the street is deserted. Relieved of its tourists and mourners, Père Lachaise closed its gates several hours ago. All that remains is the faint hum of traffic on Boulevard Ménilmontant. It is at this time of day, after dark, that Billie wishes she could go and wander along the cemetery paths, beneath the boughs of hundred-year-old trees, surrounded by the chirping blackbirds hopping between the graves. From her vantage point the mausoleums take on different faces, morphing in turn into little cottages or crouching giants.

She thinks about how she has always been drawn to this place, ever since the day she discovered it, when she first visited the flat and stood admiring the plunging view from its windows. It was winter. Pale morning light flooded the living room, illuminating the damp patches on the ceiling, the chipped paint and the shabby parquet floor. Everything would need refurbishing. But that was of little consequence compared to the charm of the sloping walls, the generous space she could create by taking down the partition wall that divided the main room in half, and above all the endless sweep of sky criss-crossed by long branches stretched out high above the graves and the mossy ground. Billie had lingered there a while taking in the view, mentally surveying the different sections of the cemetery. Then something had caught her eye: a stone female silhouette bent over one of the tombs by the cemetery wall. It was only because the trees were bare, affording her an uninter-rupted view, that she had noticed the figure. Had she visited the flat on a summer's day, she probably would have missed her. That was the moment she knew that she was going to live there.

Billie had waited until the day she moved in to pay her a visit. She had observed her from the window again, through the spring buds, noting her exact location, then had made her way to the cemetery, entering through the Porte du Repos, just behind a group of tour-ists. She had walked on, keeping close to the cemetery wall, following it until she found her: a beautiful grey figure, the ends of her veil covered in moss. The statue was of a kneeling woman bending over the tomb, a funeral wreath held firmly in each hand. She appeared to be resting her entire body weight on the wreaths, as if they were crutches. Billie had walked all the way round the tomb, before crouching down in front of it to get a better view of the face beneath the veil. The woman, her eyes half-closed, was keeping watch over the twin wreaths. She was not in fact leaning on them. Rather, she was clasping them, cradling them like two delicate creatures. Two offspring of her stone womb, Billie had thought with a shiver, real-ising what it was about this statue that troubled her.

She turns back, studies the canvas awaiting her in its halo of light, appraises her sketch from a distance. She thinks about the exhibition, about the ridiculous deadline she has agreed to. 11.30 p.m. She pours herself another cup of coffee. It's lukewarm, but its smell alone is enough to invigorate her.

Engrossed in her exploration of the face, her thumb curled around the stick of charcoal, she is touching up the lips when the telephone rings, making her jump. The charcoal jerks across the canvas, spoiling the graceful contours of the mouth.

Ruined! The misshapen mouth, spewing black powder down the chin. How on earth is she supposed to fix that? The phone keeps on ringing, shattering the drowsy atmosphere of the flat. Billie kneads the eraser, tempted to scupper the whole thing. But the moment passes. She turns away from her disfigured creation and answers the phone.

A cough, a hesitant voice:

'Hello? I'm sorry to disturb you so late. I was hoping to speak to Billie Savy.'

'Speaking.'

'Good evening, ma'am, I'm the manager of Les Oliviers. It's about your mother. There's been . . . an accident . . . I'm sorry. Louise . . .'

The words are like a hammer blow. She straightens up. The stick of charcoal snaps between her fingers.

She wonders if she might have misheard what the woman on the other end of the line is telling her, because at that moment the decrepit lift apparatus lurches into motion, and, somewhere on the landing, the parquet floor creaks under one, then two sets of footsteps. Of this – these footsteps – Billie is certain. Everything else is a blur for now. She is tempted to banish the words from her mind. *Louise* . . . Her hand, which had been holding the charcoal so firmly only a moment ago, starts to tremble, curling in on itself like an injured animal. She feels the tingle of sweat under her arms, her breathing constricted, just as used to happen before a big dive, when the water's surface looked so smooth and far away that she was almost expecting her bones to break on impact.

'Hello? Can you hear me, Miss Savy?'

Billie can hear doors banging and voices whispering in the background. She can picture the unexpected commotion down there at such a late hour on this summer night.

'A most unfortunate accident. How your mother managed to get down to the river we have no idea. After all, the whole area is properly . . .'

'The river?'

Billie had forgotten there was a river nearby. She has never seen it, but she knows it's there, well beyond the end of the gardens at the back of the main building at Les Oliviers. The residents, most of whom are getting on in years, never venture that far. On rainy days they can barely hear the sound of the water lapping. And if one of them took it into their head to approach the river, the fence running alongside it would be enough to deter them.

'Yes, the river. That's where your mother was found. I'm afraid Louise drowned.'

Her mind seizes up, blocks out the sickening words. No, it's not possible. She ought to hang up, stop listening to them – these words unleashed all of a sudden here, at home, light-years away from Louise – and then forget them. She is good at forgetting.

'But what happened? How did my mother manage—'

'We've questioned the staff who were on duty this evening. No one noticed anything different from usual. Louise was calm. She stayed in the lounge for a little while after dinner, then she went upstairs to bed. At about ten o'clock the night nurse noticed her bedroom door was open and saw that the room was empty. We searched the building for her. We checked the other bedrooms. Nobody saw her. It was as if she had . . . vanished into thin air. It was the night security guard who raised the alarm. He was out patrolling the grounds, and spotted the nightie caught on the fence.'

'The nightie?'

'Your mother's nightdress . . . It must have hitched on the fence and—'

'My God!'

Billie closes her eyes for a moment, tries to dispel the image of Louise's naked, scratched body.

'We found her in the water. Up against . . . Up against a rock.'

She hears no more after that. She couldn't care less about the condolences, the regrets and the macabre details.

Louise has drowned. That one fact is all that matters. Billie has to focus on it, assimilate it: late on 21 July, her mother drowned. On the eve of her birthday. She wasn't even sixty, although she had long since absented herself from this world.

Then there is the hideous coincidence. For Louise's freezing body in the river awakens memories of another. Its skin the same pale shade as a moon jellyfish. The face suffused with bluish purple due to the lack of oxygen in the body tissues and internal organs. Bubbles forming on the lips, a mix of inhaled water, air and bronchial mucus. A delicate foam that spreads to the nostrils once the body is lifted from the water. Bulging eyes like a fish. Goose-pimpled flesh. Billie has seen it all before. She is familiar with the bodies of the drowned.

PART ONE

Billie

I

Bill! Bill!
 The reedy voice is drowned out by the din of the river.
Hey! Bill!
It grows urgent, distorted, hoarse.
Wait for me!
Her breathing weakens, changes cadence.
Her little hand clutches at the rocks and is injured. A drop of blood gathers and hangs for a moment before falling.
Bill! Wait for me!
Diluted by the water, the ring of scarlet spreads, soaking into her blonde plaits.

Billie is woken by her own cry. She tries to make out the time on the alarm clock. 6 a.m. The sheets are soaking. She goes to the bathroom and mops her face. When had she last had this nightmare? She walks naked across the living room and stands at the window. The sun is timidly rising over the treetops of Père Lachaise. The coolness of the night lingers only briefly before giving way to the stifling heat of summer.

She casts her mind back to the telephone call of the previous night. To the words. *It's about Louise . . . The accident. The river. I'm sorry.*

The image impresses itself on her: her mother caught in the currents, her freezing body being hauled out of the water and laid, in a panic, on the riverbank. Feeling for a pulse in the dark, refusing to give up on her, while the river continues on its way unperturbed.

It is the same appalling scene that seems to be repeating itself twenty years on, like some sorry refrain. From across the years, the other body, that of someone likewise dearly loved, looms up next to Louise's. In the water their blue skins are hard to tell apart. Remorse is entwined with sorrow.

The memory of the river in V crystallises slowly in her mind's eye. Once again she sees the leafy canopy above the clear water, the carpets of moss decaying in autumn, and the hidden crannies smelling of wet earth and walkers' urine. The water hurtling along furiously between the rocks, so they had to shout to make themselves heard. Bill and Lila, both in their multicoloured swimming costumes, used to roam along the riverbank by the icy pools. It was such a long time ago. The fresh water, rocky riverbanks and damp hiding places had been their playground, their hunting ground, a place of refuge, before they became a trap.

And now her mother has drowned, in a river that is not the same river as in V, but must be similar. Louise never liked it, never went there. She preferred the warm waters of the Mediterranean sea.

Billie feels a creeping anguish, which settles as a hard lump in her throat. It's unbearable, this sudden need to take stock of the living and the dead, to recall her world as it used to be. Impossible. V and its dark temptations were such a long time ago.

Yet in a few days they will be holding Louise's funeral. She will have to go back there and shut up the house in V for good. And in burying her mother Billie will also lay everything else to rest. The joys and the follies. The knowledge of what happened. She has managed to forget it. All of it. Henri, dominating their lives one moment and absent the next. Suzanne, her tears that last summer; her howl, the chilling howl of a she-wolf that awakened the whole of the hinterland. Lila, her friend, her sister.

And Jean.

Billie goes over to the window in the hope of getting some air, to no avail. She has taken the time she needed – years of omission and absence – to purge her memory. Until that ghastly telephone call everything had been in order. Nothing remained of her past life. But Louise, with her final act, has brought everything back. The ghosts of V have returned and will sow the seeds of disorder once more. She will have to silence them and dispel any lingering traces. She will manage it. She will manage to forget once again. She has what it takes to erase things from her memory. It's purely a matter of determination.

She slips on a t-shirt, sets the coffee machine going, switches on the radio, turns up the volume, takes a mug and adds a spoonful of sugar. She sits down at her work table and gazes out at the gravestones of Père Lachaise. She turns things over in her mind, allows her thoughts to drift with the music for a while.

She needs to halt this merry-go-round before it spirals out of control. She must not let herself get carried away, not think about the river, but keep her feet firmly on the ground, stay in control, concentrate on the lines she is going to draw in the space where nothing yet exists.

She has made up her mind: she will still go along to her meeting in Rue des Rosiers. She can handle it. She will shortly be showing the gallery owner and exhibition designer her latest sketches. Her application has been accepted. She will have her own exhibition this winter. They liked the angular faces, executed entirely in charcoal, monochrome, dark and tormented: 'powerful' was how they described them. Billie was quietly thrilled and promised to get the last canvas to them by the end of the summer. She has five weeks to go. It's nowhere near long enough, but this exhibition is her golden opportunity. She has been waiting for something like this for so long.

She fingers the stick of charcoal.

The first curve slices through the white space. The outlines of the face are sketchy at first. Then the charcoal fills in the gaps. The aquiline nose takes shape, emerging from the shadow.

Lines zigzag side by side like the strands of a wire fence. Beneath the bushy eyebrows, the gaze is coming alive.

The mouth now. The line forms a smile, but then goes astray.

The smile is off. She tries to flesh it out with the aid of the eraser. A touch of light in the corners of the lips.

It's no good. Her subject is blurry. The face seems to ripple, as if under water.

Billie feels sick; she has a nagging ache in the pit of her stomach. She lets go of the charcoal and rips up the sheet.

She leans back in her chair, closes her eyes, weighs up the pros and cons and opens the drawer of the coffee table. That is where she keeps her emergency cigarettes. She eyes the cigarette between her trembling fingers for a brief moment and gives in. She lights it, inhales deeply. Her head spins slightly, but the feeling doesn't last long. She thought the buzz would be more intense. She leans towards the telephone, blows out a cloud of smoke in its direction then sucks the nicotine into the depths of her lungs one more time.

What if she were to call Paul? Tell him all there is to say? About the death of the person she never called *Mum* because Louise didn't like it. The death of the woman from V, once a pretty girl who had men turning to look at her in the street before she drove them away; the woman afraid of her own shadow; the mother, sunny-natured one moment, gloomy the next, who would lose track of time and suddenly remember she needed to go and collect her daughter – her oh so tiny daughter – from wherever she had left her.

And the rest as well. All of it. Lila. Her own cowardice. The unbearable fear. The impossibility of going back there, seeing the faces of the people of V again.

She concentrates on the number she is dialling. Just focus on that, on that number. Her fingers crush the half-smoked cigarette.

What would she say? 'Hello, Paul? It's me. My mother died last night and there's something I have to tell you. I have to tell you about where I come from. What I've done. But please don't judge me, okay? Promise me you won't judge me.'

What would he reply? 'Hey, baby, you weren't to know. If you'd known what was going to happen, you would never have done that . . . I know you, baby, trust me. Come on, there's no point dwelling on it. You can't go back to the past.'

No, a call wouldn't work. You don't just spring those kinds of things on people out of the blue. You try to soften the blow, prepare the ground.

Billie gazes at the white page in front of her. It crosses her mind that she could draw what's distressing her. Her pain. And the other pain, from further back, which is surging up again and sinking its claws into her. Perhaps giving it a precise shape would have a calming effect, at least for a while. She would sketch the six-storeyed building, its red-brick façade in the morning sun. The cemetery adjoining it. She would draw herself sitting at her work table, a wooden table-top on two trestles, in one of the top-floor windows. Passers-by in the street below, if they happened to glance up, would notice this woman, a dishevelled brunette in her thirties with her elbows propped on her table, lost in thought or concentrating on something. They would not see the storm raging inside her, would not have the slightest inkling of how her mind is racing. From above the apartment building in Rue du Repos, delicate petals would begin to fall like spring rain. Not tears, nor drops of water, but purple-tinged blossom. The flowers would unfurl beneath her brush like cloudy jellyfish. They would multiply, inundating everything, saturating the air with their sickly perfume. And Billie would disappear, swallowed up.

Yes, she would draw that: the lilac rain bringing with it the ghost of Lila – her friend, her sister – starving her of oxygen, violently propelling her towards the river and its deadly games.

Louise. Lila. Their skin blue in the water. Their bodies caught up in the treacherous currents. Past and present intertwining in a strange ballet. Fingers grasping. A fingernail torn on a rock. Hairbands pulled out, the blonde plaits set free. Is this how obsession is born?

Billie turns away from the window, goes into the kitchen and spoons more coffee into the coffee machine's filter.

Other than Paul, who could she call? There is no one. She has stuck rigidly to her self-imposed survival zone.

She casts her mind back to the drama of her arrival in Paris, and those early days when her head was in a spin. The blank faces of the passers-by had left her dumbfounded at first. Then she had got into her stride, and got into the buzz of city life. And what she had enjoyed more than anything, at least in the beginning when everything was new, was its constant hum, its teeming streets. In Paris, unlike the place she came from, there was no real silence.

When she fled V twenty years ago, she had taken with her all her savings and a single rucksack filled to overflowing. Its thread-bare straps had chafed her shoulders when she alighted from the train in Paris, tired and dirty. She had just turned seventeen and had known nothing other than the steep little streets of her village, the unchanging view of the valley and the terraced hillsides, the raging waters of the river. Billie had sat down in a café opposite the Gare de Lyon and ordered an orange juice. Perusing a newspaper she had found lying on a bench, she had spotted the advertisement: *Flatshare: room to let in a comfortable 3-roomed flat. All amenities.* She had gone along a few hours later to view it, with just enough money on her to pay her first two months' rent. The woman had opened the door and given her the once-over before inviting her in. Billie told her she was going to look for work straight away – 'any kind of work'. With her messy hair and puffy yellow-rimmed eyes, Billie had reminded the woman of a sparrow fallen from its nest. The nickname had stuck: *little bird*. The woman had shown her around the flat. 'Is that all you've got?' she had asked, gesturing at the rucksack. Billie had nodded her head. 'I'll let you sort yourself out then . . . Are you hungry?' She had nodded again. 'Come and join me in the kitchen when you're ready.'

Branching off Rue Raymond Losserand, the Rue des Thermopyles – her 'little island', as Billie would come to call it – was a quaint cobbled street lined with houses with wrought iron doors and walls painted in all the colours of the rainbow. On entering this green oasis, you felt as though you had stumbled across a patch of countryside, a kind of refuge within the city. On that first morning, though, Billie had walked down it without looking around her. She had soon spotted the house number given in the small ad, had strode into the small yellow building and darted up the slightly rickety stairs to the third floor. It was only much later that she came to appreciate the cooing of the wood pigeons, the wisteria and the Virginia creeper that twined its way from one balcony to the next.

Her landlady was twenty or so years her senior and was everything Louise had never been. Consistent. Dependable. The two of them clicked and Billie had ended up staying in the flat for seven years. The woman in Rue des Thermopyles talked a lot and didn't ask many questions. She had that remarkable ability to fill a room with her presence while also respecting the silences. 'You're not planning on being a waitress for the rest of your life are you, little bird?' she had asked Billie the day she had first caught sight of her early sketches. She had been bowled over by them and encouraged her to keep at it, to take drawing lessons. 'You just need a few pointers, Billie. To work on your technique. If you can just learn some technique, you'll be well on your way!' She had convinced her to enrol in a decent school. And Billie hadn't looked back, had become a workaholic. She had started looking for a flat of her own and, after a succession of viewings, soon fell in love with the one in Rue du Repos. It was perfect for her, as someone who couldn't tolerate confined spaces, so much a feature of the house in V.

V was a long way off.

V had faded away.

If one doesn't talk about a thing, it has never happened. Billie had read that somewhere and had followed the principle to the letter. She had made it her mantra. She wouldn't say a word about the village, the heat, the betrayals. She wouldn't speak of the hundred-year-old walls, the parched earth or the remorse. She would wipe from memory that part of the world where the sun is relentless and the hills are round, abounding with rivers engorged with water despite the searing heat. No one but she would know about the other side of the picture, the wearying summer crush, the way time is drawn out. That terrible slowness. The tedious hours dragging by in the mind of a young girl longing for adventure. In their teens, they had all dreamed of moving to the city. They thought that anything would be possible there. The village kids viewed this other place as either a welcome escape route or a mysterious threat. She, Billie, had taken the leap. She had left. She had stolen away like a thief.

Avoiding mentioning her former life was not that difficult: it became a habit with her, to say little and ask little. Maybe that way people would leave her in peace, she reasoned. But people are so inquisitive. *You're running away, Billie! Running away from questions, running away from guys, running away from your life! Even when you're standing still you still seem like you're running!* How many times had she heard that from people pretending to take an interest in her? But she had kept it up. From that point on, V no longer existed.

And now Louise . . . Louise drowns herself. On the eve of her birthday, instead of lying listening to the familiar coughs and moans of the other residents and waiting in vain for sleep to come, she sneaks out into the corridors of Les Oliviers. Dressed in her white nightie, she pads across the worn linoleum in her bare feet and somehow, no one knows how, manages to make it all the way to the river at the far end of the grounds. She hurts herself, but doesn't give up. Her final effort of will goes into scaling the fence.

How did it happen? Billie had asked on the telephone. How could something like this come about? No one knows, of course, neither the manager of Les Oliviers nor the care home staff who are supposed to keep an eye on the residents. Louise put an end to herself in the dead of night. Under a nearly full moon, her crooked body slithered like a snake down the river, hidden from view by the long grass. She wove her way through the water. At some point she forgot to breathe. Or perhaps she had wanted to do a dive, a big jump just as she used to do in her prime. And in her eagerness she simply snapped her fragile neck.

Is that how it happened? Struggling with the muddle in her

faltering mind, did she for a brief moment imagine she had become the Louise of the past again? A spell of confusion in which reality became warped. Louise dissolving as her body plunged, swept towards a different time.

The time before. The time of her childhood in the low-ceilinged house in V. The time of black butterflies and sunlight hours.

Midday already. Billie stands up. Her meeting is in less than an hour. She just has time to gather up her things and run to the metro. She throws on a thin blouse, a skirt, a pair of sandals.

An accident. An unfortunate accident. The kind of accident that can happen to fragile, ageing bodies.

And yet, as she hastily grabs her portfolio and the photographs of her latest canvases, checks the address of the gallery in Rue des Rosiers and the nearest metro station, a dreadful sense of doubt is worming its way into her mind. How did it happen, Louise? Tell me how something like this could happen to you. You who used to be such an excellent swimmer. The best in the south. You were never any good at cooking, or looking after your daughter, but you knew how to swim. I can still see you on one of those golden Mediterranean beaches. Your muscular body cuts through the water as you head towards Henri, or some other lover. Men, always. While I sit there, tearing my hair out with boredom, burying myself in the sand, you are swimming towards your lover. Impossible Louise who can't do without a man. The weight of your loneliness. And of mine.

2

Paris. Its cafés. Its bridges. The metro, a constant presence. Billie has lost count of the hours she has wasted in these tunnels teeming with odours and bodies. The clatter of metal, the shabby folding seats, the foul breath. And, mingling with all the smells, the rose spray that, rather than freshening the air, seems only to heighten the effect of the odours, leaving her with a feeling of nausea that lasts all the way to the exit.

If there were a bit more space, Billie would perhaps come to enjoy this time out. Underground travellers tend to become attuned to the rhythm of their city. They have this forced interlude down to a fine art. She observes them with interest during her moments of calm: one silently moving his lips, another noisily recounting some drama from her life, or reading something without taking it in because she keeps checking she hasn't missed her stop.

There is also the religious nut, never the same one, who is always on her evening route, as if all the crackpots in the city were coordinating with one another. She listens to him preach a message that only he understands. He speaks to her of God and the Last Judgement. Billie is sure he is addressing her, taking her to task, that he knows what she is capable of. She casts her eyes down, far down, her gaze passing right through the filthy floor of the carriage, seeking out the rails below.

This evening, it's unbearable. She has managed to thread her way through the crowd of commuters and find a space next to a door, but even there, with her nose up against the dirty window, her portfolio clenched to her stomach, she is suffocating. Her heart is racing. Is she going to start having her funny turns again?

As the train passes over the Seine, she tries to control her breathing rate. She focuses on the Eiffel Tower soaring up majestically above them. So beautiful.

Louise had long dreamed of Paris. And in the end, she had come, accompanied by the latest man in her life, George something-or-other. Billie was twenty-five at the time. She had been here for eight years, far from Louise, far from V. Eight years since they had seen each other.

It was an event in itself, the first time Billie had ever seen her mother in a setting other than V. Louise had finally ventured beyond her home territory, her native soil. And here, in these new surroundings, it struck Billie that her mother had lost some of her sparkle. Amid the crowds of people, she simply became another figure, squeezed into an evening dress that looked out of place in daylight, sitting outside a café, stiff, clutching her handbag crammed full with useless items, overly made-up and, most noticeably, incapable of summoning up one of those radiant smiles of hers that were so familiar from the good old days. That day she was already absent, as if she had withdrawn into herself. The three of them had sipped their grenadine, Billie and Louise silent as usual. Then Louise had headed off again with her man. They were going to go up the Eiffel Tower before taking the train home. Louise had turned back to look at her, had given her a wave and a look that seemed to say *Sorry, I wasn't up to it.* She could hardly hold it against her. Clearly there was no hope of putting things right in such a short space of time. They would each head off in opposite directions, the way they always did.

Then came the first signs – temporary lapses of memory, becoming ever more frequent. George had called one morning to let Billie know, to tell her about the premature onset of the disease, the fact that Louise's symptoms were unusually advanced for someone so young. Louise couldn't stay in the house any longer; it was too dangerous. They would have to find a place for her where she would be happy. Happy. The *happy* had made Billie cringe. But she couldn't exactly say anything – she who was miles away, who had never taken the trouble to return to the place where she had grown up, she who would slip away again.

The last time she had seen Louise was three years ago, in that dreary institution with the incongruous name, Les Oliviers – the olive trees. Billie had promised her at the time that she would come back, but she hadn't.

Les Oliviers. Lush green gardens. Comfortable air-conditioned rooms, each with its own shower room, plus a dining room that doubled as an activity room, a hairdressing salon, a library . . . She had read all that in the brochure before visiting. If you took that carefully crafted sales pitch at face value, you might almost be tempted to go there on holiday.

At Les Oliviers everything was white. And blue. And peaceful at first glance, although there were rooms where people were shouting, getting worked up, demanding explanations. Billie had been given various instructions before being taken to her mother's room.

The white corridor featured rows of identical doors in quite an attractive soft blue, but the fluorescent lights gave off a harsh glare, and an unpleasant smell hung in the air. The smell of medicines and of something else – she couldn't exactly put her finger on what – that had suddenly brought home to her the reality of Louise's life.

In the middle of each blue door was a card bearing the name of the occupant. *Lucie F., Jacqueline R., Lisette M.* It struck her immediately that the names on these identical doors were all names of women. Where were the men? And what would one find behind those sky-blue doors? Silvery haired women surrounded by their visiting children and grandchildren? They were so unobtrusive that there was not a sound to be heard in the corridor apart from the squelch of shoes on lino and the occasional husky cough followed by the sound of spitting.

Billie had paused outside her mother's door to catch her breath. She had been tempted to turn around and walk right back the way she had come.

'Louise?'

The silhouette outlined against the window had remained motionless, indifferent to Billie's entering her room. Billie had closed the door noiselessly behind her and placed a box of chocolates on the bed.

'Louise?'

As she moved closer, her gaze took in Louise's hair fastened in a bun, the smattering of grey strands in the lustrous mass of brown. Time could not touch her mother's impressive mane. Her pride and joy. Sitting at the window in a tight flannel blouse and a skirt that was too long for her, she was gazing out at the grounds, which extended as far as the eye could see, continuing well beyond the outer walls. 'Louise?' Billie had repeated, bending down to her level.

The woman with the bun had jumped and turned to look at her, suddenly astonished to find this person standing next to her. And Billie, too, had felt a kind of shock when their eyes met.

'Who are you?'

The voice was childlike, strangely cheerful. Louise had looked at Billie with wild eyes. She was still beautiful. Hers was an ethereal beauty. The envelope was almost intact, barely marked by time, but it was empty.

Billie had been so panicked that she had walked back out of the room. It felt as if, all of a sudden, her childhood fears were flooding back. She had paced in circles in the corridor. Where was Louise? How quickly had she slipped away? How many months, how many years had it taken before she finally relinquished everything she used to be? And if Billie had stayed in V, would the process have been slower, would they have been able to devise some daily exercises to delay the advance of the disease?

But she was there now. She needed to calm down. She had gone back into the room and sat down close to her mother. She, too, had looked out at the grounds, at the trees with their spreading branches, the birds flying freely through the air as if teasing them.

* * *

She had found a hotel and stayed for three days. An eternity. At Les Oliviers time seemed to stand still. The days were marked out only by the routine of taking medications. At the appointed times the nurses would make their way along the corridors, disappearing through each of the blue doors in turn.

With the exception of these legions of white coats, everything here proceeded at a snail's pace. If you stayed in this place too long, you did so at your peril. You could be swallowed up here – lose all sense of time, fall asleep here for ever, like Louise.

Billie had embraced the pace of life at Les Oliviers, its immobility. Sitting beside her mother at the window, she had entered into her space. Louise was so near and so far from her, focused on her own void, working ceaselessly to fill it. Billie had wondered if Louise might have a sudden flash of illumination that would rekindle the spark in her lifeless eyes and set the machine in motion once again. And everything would carry on as normal.

'Do you like flowers, Louise?' When she walked into her mother's room on the second day, Billie had proudly presented her with a bouquet. She had rummaged in the wardrobe, which contained a few items of clothing, a dressing gown, a shoebox and a mohair blanket, but not what she was looking for. A room with no vase – how sad. 'I'll just be a couple of minutes.' She unearthed a plastic glass in the bathroom, filled it with water, untied the string around the stems and spread out the flowers in an artful display. She had cast an eye around the room and in the end opted for the chest of drawers by the window.

'There you go. Do you like them?'

Billie had watched Louise as she looked at the bouquet of blooms in delicate shades ranging from pink to violet. The flowers, which each had four petals, gave off a faintly spicy fragrance.

Lilac. *Lila*.

Billie had whispered the word several times, hesitantly to start with, then she had grown used to it, even finding a certain pleasure in repeating the two long-lost, taboo syllables aloud. *Li-la. Li-la.*

She had kept going, scanning for a reaction in her mother's eyes. Could the mention of this name jolt Louise from her torpor? If only it would awaken something in her. Do you hear it? Could it bring you back to the here and now?

But her mother wasn't listening. She was leaning forward, looking out of the window with her hands folded, frowning as if she had spotted something. She was completely ignoring Billie.

'You know they cut my tree down.'

'Your tree?'

'Yes, the tree I could see from my window. They cut it down just the other day. They said it was rotten on the inside, that it sounded hollow, that it would have fallen down anyway one day.'

'Oh, I'm sorry.'

The fragile bud resisting the April frosts, the blossoming followed by the decay, the bare branches: Louise must like this spectacle of the seasons parading by in front of her; it must be enough for her.

'They said there would have been an accident. But I know that's not true. That tree was so peaceful, it never moved, so tell me, what kind of an accident could it possibly have caused?'

'It might have fallen on someone.'

'. . .'

'It might have come crashing down in a storm, for example. These things happen, you know.'

'. . .'

'Louise?'

'Yes?'

'Do you understand what I'm saying?'

'Who are you?'

'You know, the girl with the chocolates.'

'Oh yes! I like your chocolates.'

They had sat down on a bench in a shady spot in the gardens surrounding the huge building of Les Oliviers. A nurse who was passing by greeted her, then leaned towards Louise.

'Enjoying a breath of fresh air, are we? I bet you're pleased to have a visitor, aren't you?' She had patted her on the shoulder before continuing on her way.

Billie had watched the nurse walk briskly away to her next task. She didn't like the nurse's tone, the same tone that all the medical staff tended to adopt when talking to the residents. How could you not lose your identity when it was stolen from you with such gentleness? This place, these people with their honeyed voices, had they played a part in obliterating her mother? How do you weigh up the harm done, decide where the greatest blame lies?

There were all manner of activities on offer, she was told, be they practical, physical, recreational or intellectually stimulating. They included gentle exercise, bingo, pottery, handicrafts, sewing and gardening, all of which helped foster social contact. Billie had had the urge to scream as she pictured the scene: Louise sitting at a table in front of some wobbly pot that doesn't look like anything much, not that it matters because she has already forgotten what it was that she wanted to make. The Lulu of the sunlight hours has abandoned her party dresses in favour of the activity room at Les Oliviers – that gloomy space where, surrounded by her fellow sufferers, her hands covered in clay, she focuses her attention on something resembling a deformed head. *Craft activities help preserve memory function and hand-eye coordination, and, if practised regularly, are a way of maintaining social contact . . .* Bullshit! That's how Billie should have responded instead of smiling like an idiot.

It was pointless though. What difference would it make if she got worked up? She had chosen instead to follow Louise's example: to close her eyes and enjoy the last rays of sunshine over the gardens.

On the third day, before it all went wrong, they had gone downstairs to the lounge. At Les Oliviers, this consisted of a cluster of armchairs in a random assortment of shapes, sizes and fabrics, and was meant to be a place for residents to get together and have a good time. But in reality silence reigned there, and the dull drone of the television set was the only sound, interrupted once in a while by a groan or protest.

They had stopped there for a bit before their stroll in the grounds. Then Louise had felt chilly and Billie had gone back up to her room to fetch her cardigan. 'I'll be right back!' Louise had listened distractedly, her eyes on the TV screen, which showed someone getting worked up for some unknown reason.

Once in the room, Billie had had the sudden urge to go through her mother's things. The impulse had come over her in a flash: since no information would be forthcoming from Louise, she would see if she could unearth memories of the past among her belongings.

Her heart was hammering as she opened the doors of the wardrobe, fingered the clothes the way she used to as a child. She had picked up the shoebox, noticed how promisingly heavy it felt. With bated breath she had lifted off the lid and been confronted by a jumble of souvenirs: postcards, newspaper cuttings, a scribbled-on leaflet about local water-based activities, a restaurant bill. It had struck her as ridiculous that it was these items of no importance that Louise had chosen to keep after she had had her big clear-out of the house in V before moving into the pretty room at Les Oliviers. *It's nice there, you'll be happy there, and it's got huge grounds. You'll have a wonderful view from your room.* That's how they must have put it to her. *But you can't keep all that stuff, Louise. You need to take just the* bare *essentials.* In getting rid of the majority of her possessions, she had consigned the last vestiges of her memory to oblivion.

Billie had tipped the contents of the box onto the bed. Among the scattered papers and other items she had found an old polaroid – Louise and Suzanne posing arm in arm in front of an oleander bush, smiling and bare-footed, with their shoes in their hands and their towels slung over their shoulders. Suzanne, wearing a bathing costume with multicoloured stripes – you could make them out even though the colours were faded – and hot pants, had her head turned towards Louise, who had her hand in the air and was opening her mouth, probably to call out something.

Was the photo taken by Henri? What was Louise saying to him at that moment? *Wait! We're not ready!* Louise wasn't yet thirty in the snapshot; in that dress, with its straps knotted at the shoulders, she still looked like a child.

Billie had flipped the photo over. On the back was written *With Suzie.* The letters were rounded, formed by a careful hand: the tail of the 'e' flicked upwards like an eyelash and the dot of the 'i' was the shape of a bubble. Billie had recognised the handwriting, which had remained childish despite the years. Louise would grow old, but her bubbles and clumsy flicks would stand the test of time.

She had taken the items littered across the bed and put them back in the box, sighing as she gazed around the room. So was that it? It seemed there would be no story told in hushed tones at Les Oliviers, that Louise would say nothing about her childhood. Her mother would deny all knowledge of V, as she herself had done. Everything would stay buried behind her lifeless eyes.

Billie had left the room. All in all, this bare room bore a certain similarity to the two of them: two tongue-tied, silenced beings. Incapable of hugging each other.

Later on they had sat at the window once more, commenting again on the damage done, the gap left behind: where once there had been a large spreading tree there was now a void.

'Here, would you like another one?' Billie had asked, taking the lid off the box of chocolates.

'I don't know. I'm not sure I should.'

She had covered her mouth with her wrinkled hand in a display of childish vanity. In that fleeting gesture Billie saw a perfect flash of the old Louise. Time dilated and contracted in a split second, conflating the room at Les Oliviers and the bedroom in V into one – the bedroom with the little balcony, the rumpled sheets, the creased clothes spilling out of the drawers, the stale air reeking of cheap perfume, the lipsticks and powders in all the colours of the rainbow.

'You know you like them. You should take one before I finish the whole lot.'

Louise had picked a heart-shaped one. She had chewed it with concentration as she looked out at the grounds.

'I used to have a tree. It was there, just outside the window. And then one day some men turned up with big chainsaws and chopped it down. Cut clean through it. Just like that. *Boof!* It was diseased, apparently. Yet it was so beautiful. If only you'd seen it . . .'

'I know, Louise. It's true, it was beautiful.'

'Did you see it? Did you see my tree?'

Her mother had turned towards her, alarmed by this revelation.

'You told me about it, don't you remember? Yesterday . . .'

'I like your chocolates. And—'

Louise was leaning over the box again. She looked studious all of a sudden. As she took another chocolate, the sleeve of her blouse slipped back and it was then that Billie noticed the puffy white line running from her wrist to the palm of her hand. The scar was there in full view – in all its ugliness – taunting her, reminding her that those things really had happened. That V had existed.

In a way this mark that Louise kept hidden under her sleeve, and which she used to conceal with powder, gave them something to latch on to today: oblivion would not prevail.

'Louise, I'm off now. To Paris, remember? But I'll be back soon. Do you understand? I'll be back.'

'Will you bring me chocolates?'

'Yes, I'll bring you chocolates. It's a promise,' Billie had said.

She had stroked her mother's hair. Her fingers had glided over her frail shoulder. And then she couldn't help herself. Her hand had slid all the way down to the wrist. It had come to rest at the place where the skin bulged and her fingers caressed it. Billie had lingered too long over the scar. The reaction, when it came, was as terrible as it was unexpected. The cry had shattered the silence of Les Oliviers.

'Go away!'

Louise's whole body had tensed up, mustering remarkable strength. Her anger had burst forth in a split second, exploding as it should have done twenty-five years ago rather than lying dormant.

'Go away! Bad girl!'

She was shouting angrily, her arms thrashing furiously in the air, battling an invisible enemy. Billie had tried to talk to her, calm her down, but her mother was trapped in a different time and place. She scratched at the inside of her wrist, worked at the old scar as if to tear it open a second time and purge it of its contents.

Billie had leaned on her with all her weight to keep her in her armchair and stop her from hurtling forward.

'Adele! Bad girl!'

She kept on shouting, her mind a muddle.

'It's me. It's Billie. Come on, please calm down!'

If only Louise had been able to find her way back to the padded hush of Les Oliviers. Then they would have been able to say their goodbyes properly. But Billie could already hear the commotion outside the door.

An army of nurses had entered the room, equipped to the teeth. Billie was staggered by the absurdity of the scene: four strapping figures grappling with a woman frail as a flower. They laid her on the bed, seized her wrists and ankles and brandished a syringe.

It was no use trying to bring her back to the here and now. Louise had gone. She was elsewhere, far from Les Oliviers, in the corridor of the house in V with its bare lightbulb, standing in front of her little daughter, whose bare head was reminiscent of a tree in winter.

The shouting was still going on as Billie fled. She had sought refuge, trembling, in her car, alarmed by this sudden incursion of their past into the emptiness of Les Oliviers. That is how they had parted – violently. Three years had passed since that episode. In the meantime, after two devastating storms, the new millennium had been ushered in. And Billie had not gone back.

★   ★   ★

Go away! The shouts have come back to haunt her. In the metro they mingle with the squeals of the rails. Billie clamps her hands over her ears. She focuses her attention on her heartbeat, but it's too late – she is already caught up in her own panic. She feels the damp patches under her arms and on her back, the cold sweat on her forehead. 'Are you all right, miss?' someone asks. She has to get out of there. She threads her way through the crowd, pushing and elbowing the passengers as she goes. She hears the angry reactions just as the metal doors slam shut. *Bad girl!*

3

She is looking in the mirror, mascara brush in one hand. Paul called; he is going to come over. He should be able to get away, he said. Billie put on a front, acted as if there had been no drama, as if nothing had changed. But when he is there, when he takes her in his arms, when she utters those four words – *my mother has died* – when she says them without looking at him, what will happen? What will happen to the tears massing in her throat?

While she waits, she contemplates the gloomy face in front of her. Greyish shadows form hollows beneath her eyes. Are the dark butterflies already resurfacing? Hidden away somewhere, the black-winged battalion is on the move, just starting to stir now before taking flight. It will soon be upon her, ready to topple the slightly lopsided tower that is her life.

She doesn't have the energy to do a full make-up job, so she settles for the minimum: a sweep of blusher to bring some warmth to her cheeks, a shimmery eyeshadow and a stroke of eyeliner to light up her eyes. In any case he is barely going to be looking at her.

He ought to be there by now. Would he let her know if he had been delayed again?

She has plugged in the fan, placed her mobile phone close by and is lying down. There's no escaping the heat under the zinc roofs. She waits in the semi-darkness for the stirred air to cool her down.

Maybe he will call her on the landline. She stands up, lifts the handset and listens for the dialling tone. It's working fine.

She pulls the telephone lead out of the socket and plugs it

back in again. She calls her mobile phone from the landline. It rings over and over in the silence. She tries again several times.

All she can do is wait.

Four years already. She wishes she had never met him. Has she really wasted four years waiting for him? The days were sweltering then, just as they are now. Paris was stifling. It was a summer punctuated by dramatic thunderstorms similar to those in V – downpours as glorious as they were sudden, a familiar feature of her childhood. She had drunk and danced all night at a bar near the Bastille, then returned home exhausted and unsteady in the pleasantly cool air of the dawn hours. Billie remembers that night in minute detail: the shivers running up and down her legs, the moment she lost her balance and leant against him. He had slipped a bit of paper into her skirt pocket, against her damp thigh, as she was dancing. She had fiddled with it, smiling, still reeling slightly from the encounter a few moments before, from the taste of those lips – something unfamiliar to her just a few hours earlier, but which suddenly was all she could think about. Desire can invade everything in no time; you need only let your guard down for a few seconds.

After a short night she had dragged herself to the kitchen, her head throbbing, having had not a wink of sleep. *That's the last time I let myself go like that!* She made the same vow every time.

The heat was unbearable. She had downed a large glass of water to cool her burning throat, forced herself to have an ice-cold shower. Then she had switched on the fan and attempted to make a start on her work. That had kept her preoccupied for a while. It was just as well: it meant she no longer noticed the hours rolling by; she could forget about the bit of paper slipped into her skirt pocket. She could no longer remember the man's name. Only his lips, which she could still feel on hers, like a bite.

Her stomach was rumbling. She had cut up a tomato and slung the pieces in a bowl with a dash of rapeseed oil and vinegar. Recalling the ring the man had been wearing on his left hand, she had cast a sideways glance at the skirt dropped at the foot of the sofa – and had cracked. She had picked it up and fished out the crumpled bit of paper from the pocket. The ink was smudged, but you could still read his name and telephone number. She had forgotten he was called Paul; his lips were all she could think of. She had taken an avocado, peeled off the brittle skin and cut the flesh into rough chunks, then quickly mixed every-thing together. The result resembled a kind of mush. She had taken her time over each spoonful – it's important to eat slowly, the nutritionist had told her. It's important that the mind registers that you are eating, otherwise there's not enough time for a feeling of fullness to set in. But she wasn't hungry. She had thrown away the remaining contents of the bowl and eyed the two objects in front of her: her telephone and the slip of paper. She had caved in and dialled the number. Listening to the ringing against her ear, she had prayed that he would answer, and that he wouldn't answer – because what would she say to him? When he picked up, she had liked the crack in his voice. He was going to come over. All she had to do was wait.

That's what she has been doing ever since: steadfastly waiting for him. She should have known that this affair was going nowhere for her. Up until then she had held firm to the principle of sex, but not love. She knew that love leads only to chaos, that it can make you lose your mind. That it can annihilate everything that is precious to you.

But with Paul she can't help it, she can't stop herself. Does she love him? Now, at this moment, she hates him. Yet when he arrives, when he takes her in his arms, telling her that she's the only one who counts, that nothing else matters, she believes him, because of the look on his face, that earnest expression he has all of a sudden.

He desires her, there's no doubt about that. They work well together, the two of them. The slightest touch and all her senses are on high alert. Except that before long Billie disappears. She can no longer make out the outlines of her own body – her very being dissolves, and instead comes to inhabit Paul's space, where she can read his desires, feel them in the pit of her stomach, slip into them. Like him she becomes obsessed with the bodies of other women, the ones who flaunt themselves, a cheap turn-on. Like him she undresses them, imagines their hips, their breasts. Like him, she checks them out, sizes them up. And while she is Paul, while her eye is lingering on the body of another woman, her own body is eclipsed, takes a back seat, despite the furious, seething voice in her head: *I'm here!*

'Welcome to my place!'

She had had a big clear-up before his first visit, four years ago. Now stripped of its clutter, her flat was barely recognisable as hers any more. The old sofa made a strange contrast with the polished parquet floor, but the overall effect was amazing. One section of wall was still chock-full, the one where she had piled her paintings in size order so they wouldn't topple over at the slightest draught. This temporary arrangement – those towers of paper so precariously balanced – mirrored her own situation.

'Would you like a glass of wine?' she had asked, heading towards the kitchen.

'Sure.'

Ensconced on the sofa, which sagged perilously under his weight, Paul was surveying every corner of the flat.

'Have you read them all?' he had asked, pointing to the book-case.

'What? The books? No, not all of them.'

'What are you reading at the moment?'

'I'm re-reading! I'm getting back into Maupassant. I'm discovering another side to him. It's a long time since I last—'

'And what are you discovering?'

He had clinked his glass against hers.

'Well, what I remember is *A Life* – its descriptions, the slow pace of it. But now I'm really taken by *The Horla*. The writing is more anguished. It's a different Maupassant. Kind of crazy. I like him like that.'

The alcohol was starting to take effect and helping to calm

her nerves. Butterflies in the stomach, the trademark of lovers-
to-be, Billie thought, as she swirled the wine in the bottom of
her glass. They hadn't talked much that evening. He had leant
in towards her, caressed her and laid her down on the rickety
sofa. They had made love. The canvases stacked against the wall
behind them looked on disapprovingly.

'Shit! It's ten o'clock already! I'm late! Shit, shit!'
    Paul had sprung to his feet, flung his shirt on inside out, then
taken it off and put it on again. His flattened hair and crumpled
clothes made him look like a scarecrow. Billie had stifled a laugh.
    'Don't you want something to eat before you—?'
    'Haven't got time!'
    'I've prepared a nice—'
    'Haven't got time!'
    'What? You've got a meeting now, at this hour?'
    'Huh? No! Why?'
    'No reason. I was just wondering . . .'
    'Okay. I'll call you.'
    Billie would have liked to say something more – anything – but
he had already banged the door closed behind him.
    She had sat on her own and eaten the dinner she – someone
who never cooked – had gone to the trouble of preparing. *Arsehole!*
She had vowed that would be the first and last time she slept
with him. She had thrown the dinner leftovers in the bin. The
next day she couldn't help checking the screen of her telephone
every so often. The following day the waiting was worse. On the
third day she thought she was losing her mind. As she showered,
dressed, applied blusher to her cheeks, swung her flat door closed,
Billie could think about that and nothing else. Her all-consuming
new passion. She couldn't seem to escape the feel of his arms
and the smell of his body.

He is part of the furniture now. Little by little he has come to
inhabit her space, even when he's not there: the old sofa where
they would lounge on sunny Sundays, which is collapsing under

their weight but which she doesn't want to replace, the tiny balcony outside the two living room windows where she has managed to grow a tomato plant. That condescending smile when he spotted it: 'What are those, Billie? Those red things?' She has always lived alone in the flat in Rue du Repos. She likes her double-sized living room facing due south, her original parquet floor with the odd dent in it, which is bathed in light in summer, her bedroom overlooking the courtyard with its cooing pigeons, and the en-suite bathroom – such a shambles with its clutter of lipsticks, mascaras and floral fragrances. But the kitchen is definitely her favourite room, even though she doesn't cook. It's open-plan and spacious enough to eat in, hang out in. Billie had a solid-wood high table installed there, fixed to the wall, with two bar stools. She likes to sit there to draw. Sketchbook in hand, she wanders from room to room as though roaming the flat could help her think. She savours her morning interludes, perched on one of the stools. Beyond the misty windows, the sun is rising timidly over Père Lachaise. Outside, the city is still slumbering and Billie likes to imagine that she is the only one already awake, and that when she closes the front door behind her she will find nothing but empty streets. As deserted as her flat.

And then he is there, slightly late every time, with his reddish cheeks, his curly, greying hair, his sparkling smile. His smile, his disarming smile always. He comes straight from his seminars, with his shirt collar undone and his tie in his hand. He flings his suit jacket on the sofa and puts on an old t-shirt. As he is opening a bottle of wine, she asks him one or two questions, pretends to be interested in what he tells her, but the things she is desperate to ask him she keeps to herself. What have you been up to? Have you really been spending your days trawling those conferences? And what about your nights? How have you spent your nights?

Billie doesn't think about his wife – the one he is in the process of divorcing, so he's told her. She thinks about the others, the ones he comes across at his seminars. The temptation. Some would be quivering at the sight of him, Billie knows. All it would take would be for him to flash one of his smiles.

The obsessive jealousy, the sense of an imminent threat: the truth is, she has been unable to shake them since V. *D'you want to know what he did to me, Billie? D'you want to know what Jean did to me?* It's always that same uncertainty that takes root in her – swells and engulfs her – so that she is unable to withstand it. It's like a wave, a powerful breaker that prevents her from thinking straight. She is with Paul and she is trying to smell the scent of other women on him. She sniffs his neck, searches his pockets for some kind of evidence. Even though she is not the cuckolded wife. But she can't help it; she can't stop herself. No amount of reasoning can suppress the voice inside her head that has been nagging her for the last twenty years. *Tell me, Lila. Go on, tell me more. Tell me about him.* She tries to silence it by concentrating on other things: Paul's hands on her skin, the suddenly conspicuous mess in the bedroom, the smell of the warm croissants he has brought with him, the sounds from the street. And in the end, the burning obsession retreats back inside her.

It's mid-evening already. Billie looks at her watch, hesitates to call Paul. He should be there with her. Even if he said nothing – after all, no words have the power to undo or change things – his presence alone would soothe her. She's beginning to feel annoyed at him. Which is not fair, of course, as he doesn't yet know about the accident, about Louise. But when they spoke on the telephone earlier, shouldn't he have realised – from the sound of her voice, from her silences – that something terrible had happened? She always thought that in such circumstances an invisible distress signal would pass between those who love each other.

If that were the case, she too ought to have known, ought to have sensed what was going on last night, hundreds of miles away, while she was at work on her canvas. Somehow or other she ought to have heard her mother's last breath.

What are they going to do with her body? What are they going to dress her in before they lay her in her coffin? Who is going to choose her outfit? Will they do her hair, her make-up? She feels like calling them there and then to explain that they need to pay particular attention to Louise's hair, that they need to smooth it down and spread it out around her face like a halo of light.

All at once she feels a pressing need to see her mother's body. To check they haven't made a mistake, to make sure everything they have told her is true. It's possible that the woman on the telephone was mistaken. Sometimes people pronounced dead wake up. These things happen.

She feels a pain in her gut. She opens the window, leans on the railing. She watches the few passers-by down below, their outlines in the fading light, and wonders where they are heading, whether they are returning home to their families or going away.

The telephone breaks the silence in her flat. She hurries to answer it, but stops short at the last moment and waits for the answerphone to cut in.

'Billie . . . I'm so sorry, Billie. The funeral . . . It's on Thursday . . . I hope you get my message . . . Call me . . . Please, Billie.'

That voice. She shudders. How did Suzanne get hold of her number? Especially as she is ex-directory. Then again it's easy enough to track someone down – particularly in these circumstances. She can imagine the syrupy voice of the manager of Les Oliviers, her eagerness to please: *The daughter of the deceased? Yes, of course, I've got her number in Paris, I can give it to you straight away. Okay. Have you got something to write with?*

Suzanne. The one she dubbed 'the fishnet woman'. The mother hen who watched over both of them. Who suffocated Lila with love.

She breathes in hard; her heart is pounding in her chest. Like an automaton, she collects up the plates and fills the sink to the brim. The cutlery disappears, submerged beneath the mounds of bubbles on the surface of the soapy water. As she is vigorously scrubbing at one of the plates, it slips from her fingers and falls back into the sink. Billie yelps in surprise and looks down at her sodden t-shirt. She quickly pulls out the plug, grabs a tea towel and mops up the puddles as the sink empties with a glugging. She clutches her wet hand to her stomach: something in the gurgling water has snagged her attention. It comes back to her, like a spasm. The torrent rushing along between the rocks, the mighty thundering of it, the powerful, ceaseless current that demanded all your strength if you weren't to be swept away.

Nothing can resist the onslaught of the water. It steals into crevices, invades everything, even enclosed spaces. All it takes is a crack invisible to the naked eye, an unknown weakness. Nothing can escape the river.

The vision flashes before her eyes again: Louise's body, naked, washed up on a rock. She wishes she could banish that image from her mind for ever.

She closes her eyes. Behind her shut eyelids, the other body appears on the scene. Lila is splashing around in the river, making concentric circles on the water, which spread out, disturbing the flat surface of the pools and creating a kind of chaos.

And she hears the thin voice floating above the waters. It echoes in her head.

You're on, Bill!

A whisper at first – *It'll be our secret, okay?* – growing louder and more shrill.

Pinky promise! Cross my heart and hope to die, stick a needle in my eye!

She is tempted to cover her ears until it stops.

Hey Billie! Bi-i-llie! Biiiill!

Dear God, make her shut up.

Soaked through and nauseous, she stands motionless at the sink, waiting for the image of the river to recede. She gazes at her hands, which are trembling, and haven't stopped trembling since the call the previous day. She knows that if she stays put, if she doesn't go back to V, her hands will carry on shaking like two foreign bodies, helpless and out of control.

Behind her, her mobile phone vibrates and plays a familiar little jingle. She picks it up, reads the message from Paul. *Can't make it this evening. Stuck in the office. Sorry, baby. I'll call you!*

PART TWO
Bill

I

Billie recognises that particular mugginess in the air, the salty waft when the automatic doors at the airport open in front of her. She doesn't need to linger and take in the scene because she knows it like the back of her hand. Her mind seems to keep the memories stored somewhere, releasing them when the time is right: the smell of the oozing tarmac, the palm tree outlined against the blue of the sky – a uniform blue like a monochrome canvas – followed by a row of matching palm trees, the coconut scent of sun cream. The heat produces a haze that hangs over the pavements and distorts everything in sight, nibbles at the outlines of the figures in swimming trunks and flip-flops, the wet torsos blow-dried in a matter of moments by the mistral, which sweeps across the landscape, shatters the sleepy atmosphere, scoops up items in its path and whisks away voices and the chirping of crickets. Nothing has changed, then.

She has decided to hire a car for four days. With luck she will be able to return it earlier than agreed, but if the worst comes to the worst it will be her means of escape. Before collecting the keys from the hire company, she stops at the airport restaurant and orders a strong coffee. Her stomach can't handle any food. Since the previous day, all her thoughts have been focused on V.

The drive shouldn't take more than two hours. She will seek out a hotel in one of the villages she will be passing through on the way and have a quick shower before the ceremony.

★   ★   ★

She has half-opened her window, and sea spray lashes her face as she drives along the coast road. The pink villas clinging to little rocky islands glint above the pristine sea. Further out, cruise ships glide past, silent and imposing. She surveys the tranquil panorama and draws some peace of mind from it. Then she turns onto the main road leading inland, leaving the turquoise sea behind and heading into the heart of the countryside.

The road winds its way through the hilly landscape, gradually gaining altitude. Billie follows it round one bend after another, and eventually she spots the first village perched on a hillside, with its church tower silhouetted against the sky.

It's all there, intact. Time seems to be switching into reverse, running backwards. She sees herself as she was, a youngster with scratched legs and grubby knees. A tomboy weaving her way among the charred tree trunks, her cheeks bathed in sweat and tears, roaming wild in the hills singed by forest fires during the scorching summers, as if this wasteland were part of her kingdom – a lush, aromatic kingdom that before long would rise again from its ashes.

Caution! Falling rocks! She leans forward to catch a glimpse of the safety netting strung across the rock face. The road climbs steeply here and she changes gear. From the comfort of her air-conditioned car, she is reminded of the chugging of the old bus that would pick them up, her and her classmates, every morning from the bus stop at the bottom end of the village. They could hear it coming from far off, struggling along, until, by some miracle, it pulled up next to them, its engine wheezing, ready to give up the ghost.

They were eight years old. She and Lila used to travel to school together. The first few times they were accompanied by one of their mothers, who had arranged to take it in turns, but now they were big enough, responsible enough to make the journey on their own. In the afternoons they would walk along the road in single file to the bus stop, and the hot draught from the cars would make their hair fly up. They stuck their arms out above the tall grass, and the pointy tips tickled their hands. The school day was finished at last! The desks where they slouched and toiled, forgotten.

Then, in the distance, they would hear the drone of the bus that would take them home. For the children of the outlying villages, school was several miles from home. It wasn't as far as the crow flies, but the roads were very winding. That poor engine, working flat out morning and evening, spewing out fumes as it struggled uphill! When the bus opened its narrow doors, the rusty hinges would hiss like a weary animal. The girls rushed to the seats at the back and Lila and Billie, huddled up side by side, would take stock of their day at school. Both had something to say, and it came down to whoever shouted louder. They shattered the peace of the hills. The driver of the old bus seemed indifferent to the hullaballoo behind him, and Billie and her friends likewise ignored him. He was there and his presence seemed as natural as that of the dirt tracks or the church tower. He was born there, sitting behind the big black steering wheel.

The schoolchildren would say goodbye in the main square and go their separate ways until the following morning. They all went off in different directions, sometimes in twos, their school bags laden with homework assignments.

Later, once she had got her homework out of the way, Billie would go into Louise's bedroom and watch her put on her make-up. She was curious to understand how it was done, that sleight of hand. How long had it taken Louise to learn to embellish her skin like that, to tie back her hair or get it to fan out like a bouquet of flowers? She was good at painting her lips and eyelids. The glitter eyeshadow she chose made her eyes sparkle and appear a different colour. Her lips became a glistening heart. On those occasions Billie thought her mother was the most beautiful woman ever to have walked the streets of their village. She sat still on the bed and watched in silence so as not to spoil the magic of this exquisite transformation. She wanted to learn that strange art. But Louise had finished. She touched her lips to Billie's forehead in a quick kiss, clip-clopped down the stairs in her heels and shut the door behind her with an unnecessarily loud bang. Later on, as Billie slumbered, sounds would filter through from the other side of the wall, intermingled breathing, panting, the cry, the rustle of clothes, the sound of footsteps – other footsteps – going down the stairs, the click of the latch, the door slamming shut because of the draught from the alley.

Billie parked the car in the third village on her route. In the first two, the hotels had signs showing no vacancies. The coastal hinterland is extremely busy in the summer season, and the few hotels and family guest houses it has are full to capacity. The area was still undiscovered when she lived there, but these days mass tourism seems to have taken over. Now the hills are teeming with second homes. The V she knew probably no longer exists.

She stands still for a moment, puts down her travel bag and takes a look at the dingy façade, the slightly wonky sign. The place looks shabby from the outside, but it doesn't matter; she isn't here on holiday. In any case it must be the only hotel here. She walks through the entrance, notices the bar adjoining the tiny dining room and the handful of customers sitting at the tables, and collects her keys from reception.

Entering her room, she tries to ignore the yellowish marks on the wall by the bedhead, the hairs caught in the shower plughole and the stains on the old bedspread. She rolls the latter into a ball and stuffs it in the bottom of the tiny wardrobe. She avoids looking at the sheets, but instead turns her mind to the various trips back and forth that she is planning to fit in over the next three days. She calculates that she must be about twenty kilometres from V. It's perfect.

She jumps in the shower, keeps it on cold and turns it up to full pressure. The jets of water pummel her body and she relaxes for a moment. She puts on some beige trousers, a t-shirt and sandals. As she plaits her hair to make sure it will dry in an orderly fashion, she wonders whether her face has changed – whether, were it not for her crazy hair, she could go unnoticed there. If she passed someone from V, would they recognise her? With her pale skin and her yellow-rimmed eyes hidden behind sunglasses, would she be just another stranger strolling around the village streets? A distant memory, her name long forgotten? A tourist like any other?

Tomorrow she will go to Les Oliviers. She will collect her mother's personal belongings, as a daughter is supposed to. Then she will go to the house in V. Shuddering at the prospect, she opens the hotel room window and leans out. Below, everything is deserted. The village seems devoid of life. All the medieval villages around here look alike with their little squares, their dead-end streets with tall buildings on either side and their church towers looking out over the valleys. The old folk sit impassively outside their sun-scorched wooden front doors and brave the mistral, the vicious wind that can drive you to distraction.

In the streets of V, accented voices rang out, floating in the air above sun-wizened skins. But down on the ground, in the cracks of the old carriage entrances, cockroaches, giant ants, scorpions and firebugs scurried in search of welcome shade. After the sunlight hours, the twilight brought masses of fleeting silhouettes, milling around in a hum of whispers.

She pictures the house, the nest in which they co-existed, each dependent on the other. Its irregular beams, its thick stone walls with spiders' webs strung across the nooks and crannies, swathing whole areas. Upstairs the only room with its own little balcony was Louise's. It looked out onto the alley.

The house in V also had the heady odour of an old trunk, of mothballs and worn wool. In winter it smelled of cinders. All these smells clung to her, because, having been shut up inside there for so long, their skins were impregnated with them. But Billie doesn't have time to dwell on that; time is getting on. The ceremony is starting in less than an hour. She picks up her bag, leaves the key with the receptionist and gets back in the car.

* * *

Billie is eight years old. It is summer at the house in V, and her school holidays are spent roaming the fields and bathing in the river. She has come home grubby, scratched by brambles, her knees covered in mud. She has quietly shut herself in Louise's bedroom, while downstairs Louise is preparing the same old soup she always makes.

She scrutinises her figure in the mirror opposite the window. She does not like the way she looks. She despairs at her skinny body. She has the frame of a boy. Her only feminine feature is her tousled hair which falls over her shoulders. And her eyes. Yellow-rimmed eyes – captivating to some, repellent to others.

She looks like some kind of gnome – a wild thing from a place where there is nothing but dry earth and gravel that gets under your nails. She has become one with this part of France. Its fallow land, its beating sun, its narrow streams of water running dry beneath the greenery are all part of her. Now, stepping closer to the mirror, she can make out the scars on her chin and by her right eyebrow, the tangles in her hair, the dried salt on her cheeks.

Sometimes, when she is alone, when Louise is not there, she likes to transform herself, escape from her own body. She opens the wardrobe, pushes apart the dresses hanging there in order to see them better. The hangers clatter against each other. She rifles through the drawers, touches the fabrics, the lace and the silk; picks up the bottle of perfume on the chest of drawers and sprays some on herself. She gets out all the make-up, opening item after item, takes the lids off the lipsticks and creates a rainbow of colours on the back of her hand and on her eyelids. She draws a red line around her lips, puts on one of her mother's blouses and pads it out with rags. She takes a brush and makes two pink circles on her cheeks. Thus disguised, Billie performs a twirl in front of the bedroom mirror. She looks like Pierrot. A mini female Pierrot. And her child's face has become strangely un-childlike.

'Bill! Dinner's ready!'

She skips out of the bedroom and hurries downstairs. She hates that nickname. *Bill*. She hates her mother calling her that.

'Louise! Soup, in this heat? Do you want to kill us all?' exclaims Uncle Henri.

'Don't be silly! Anyway the nights are cool.'

'This must be the first time I've ever eaten hot soup in high summer.'

'Billie and I do it all the time, don't we, Billie?'

Louise gives her a wink.

For a moment, only the sounds of slurping fill the silence.

'You know what I read about that?' Louise asks.

'What? About soup?'

'About eating hot food when it's hot weather.'

'Tell me.'

'Well, apparently, when it's hot weather, it's good to drink hot drinks because that reduces the temperature difference between your body and the outside.'

'So?'

'So as a result, the temperature difference is smaller, which makes the heat feel less oppressive,' she says, sure of herself.

'You should choose something better to read . . .'

Before Louise has time to protest, Henri turns to Billie.

'What are you doing? Why aren't you eating?'

She is busy peering into her bowl and concentrating on something.

'I'm picking out the letters I need.'

'The letters?'

Henri leans closer to her. The tiny pasta shapes floating in the soup are swollen and ready to melt in the mouth. Billie fishes out a few of them, and pushes six of them to the rim of the bowl with her spoon. O, L, I, U, E, S.

'What are you writing, Billie?'

'Louise!' she says.

'Louise?'

'Yes!'

She opens her mouth wide, studies the contents of her spoon before slowly bringing it to her lips. Her tongue comes out to meet it. She examines the six swollen shapes as if she wanted to imprint the image on her memory, before swallowing the spoonful in one go. A thick, green droplet escapes from the corner of her lips.

'I'm eating Louise!'

I'm eating Louise! Which one of them ate the other in the end? Didn't they both devour each other?

Her mother's body is now surrounded by flowers and singing, with the occasional audible sob. She would have liked that – being mourned in this way. 'This is my body which is given for you.' The voice resounds beneath the vaulted roof of the church. The parish priest draws an invisible sign of the cross with the host. The congregation bow their heads. He walks forward now, in his white cassock, ready to receive them.

Trembling, Billie watches the dark figures file out of their pews and past the coffin on their way up to the altar. From where she is sitting she cannot recognise them. She can see only their backs, moving in single file, one behind the other, waiting to receive the body of Christ. But there is a chance one of them might turn round to try to catch a glimpse of something and notice her, so she retreats a little further behind the pillar.

She slips away before the mass has ended and walks to the main square in the village. She knows the cortege will pass that way. She sits down in the shade of a tree, on the little stone wall bordering the square. All she has to do is wait.

She always used to sit there with Lila and the others once the summer weather had arrived. All through the hot months, pale tourists would appear as if by magic in cars crammed to bursting. Arriving from their far-flung cities, they would file into the village, one behind the other, in much the same way she and her friends did on their return from school. After the sluggish winter months, the drag of the dead season – legs shivering in woolly tights, doors double-locked and heating on full blast – they were now free to roam again. They would run to the main square, sit in a line in their pinafore dresses on the low stone wall, and listen. They would let themselves be whisked away by the exotic voices of the pale tourists, suddenly transported to foreign shores by those accents, those incomprehensible languages which spoke to them of distant lands.

The line of mourners now appears, beneath a timid sun, following the hearse. From where she is sitting Billie can watch them without them seeing her. She moves back a little all the same. There are ten or so of them accompanying Louise to her final resting place. The 'star' will have a modest send-off. The world at large won't have heard the news. *May your soul rest in peace.*

Behind her sunglasses she averts her gaze. She knows they are there, that Suzanne, too, is walking along behind the hearse. Billie can't see her, but she knows her tears, her hysterical weeping, only too well. The last thing she wants is to be subjected to that again.

She stays put for a moment after the tiny procession has passed. Her blood is still pounding in her temples. It has all happened so quickly, this sudden reappearance of V in her life. The work of forgetting is long and painstaking; it requires such vigilance. And now, after all this time, here she is, at the scene of her childhood, surrounded by her ghosts and trying to evade them.

And then, just as she is on the point of leaving, she notices him – a solitary figure further back – and her heart skips a beat. Rather than his slightly stiff gait, which has not changed over the years, it is his red hair that catches her eye. She would recognise it anywhere.

It's him, that man who is hanging back, following the others at a distance. So he knows and has come back. *Uncle Henri.* The man who was sometimes there and sometimes not, coming and going according to whim, like the rain or the wind. He has come back to say his official goodbyes to Louise. Silent, hidden goodbyes, like Billie's.

Henri used to visit them during the summer season. Before his arrival the whole house was turned upside down, as Louise energetically cleaned the place from top to bottom, opened the

windows, let the air and the light in. She took all their savings
and filled the kitchen cupboards with endless tins and jars. She
became the good fairy who transformed the house with a wave
of her wand.

It is summer. Uncle Henri is coming, and he is going to relieve
the monotony of V, dispel Louise's sadness. Fruit appears in the
house, its flesh ready to explode in your cheeks. There are bowls
full of green, red and yellow vegetables and Billie makes off with
the odd one. They dust the place, send the spiders running,
destroy their webs. And her mother sends her out to pick wild
flowers, which she puts in vases all around the house.

This is why she likes Uncle Henri. Because with him, Louise
is a different person. When he is there they go for walks across
the fields Billie knows so well. And she is no longer the only one
roaming around there. She hears her uncle's breathing behind
her – he is not used to these long sprees. Louise has made a
picnic, which they eat in the shade of an olive tree, the three of
them sitting around the edges of the blanket. Louise is cheerful.
They dance. Louise whirls around, but her movements are
strange, slightly faltering.

When they arrive home in the late afternoon, they drive in
Henri's swanky car to one of the neighbouring villages, and have
dinner in a square with a gushing fountain. They eat their meal
to the sound of its splashing, and Billie thinks about the next
day. About the river. About Lila.

But Louise's transformation was not the sole reason Billie looked
forward to his visits. He was also the only man who took an
interest in her. The others stole away in the middle of the night
before she had even had a chance to see their faces. If ever one
of them did happen to pass her in the corridor, he would immediately hurry away as if she were a leper.

Uncle Henri always brought her a surprise when he came,
though it wasn't really a surprise any more as she knew what
it would be: it was always a china doll with painted cheeks.

She had a whole collection now. These traditional dolls, he told her, came from the town where he lived in Alsace. At the time Billie wondered whether the women in Henri's part of the country looked like the dolls, whether they had that same white skin tone.

'Hurry up, Billie! I need you to clear up all this mess. And go and get some flowers. We should at least have some flowers on the table for when he gets here. Come on, get a move on! My God, look at the state of this house. You can hardly move for clutter. Come on, look lively!'

It is a Sunday and she is eleven. She comes back from the fields with armfuls of flowers. Her hair has begun to grow back, quicker than Lila's. From a distance they still look like two boys. Lila spends her time complaining and hiding what remains of her hair under ridiculous bandeau headbands. Billie makes fun of her. It may not have turned out as planned, but it was worth the try.

Her uncle greets her with a broad smile, lifts her up and gives her a hug. Billie finds it hard to deal with these sudden shows of affection – there is too long a gap between his visits. She forgets the smell of him.

'My, how you've grown, Billie! Last time you were only this tall. See, you came up to here on me. You're a proper young lady now. Come this way, I've got something for you. But on second thoughts, I'm not sure I can give it to you. You're far too big!'

'Oh yes you can, Uncle Henri! It's fine for any age!'

He bursts out laughing. She feels his sturdy hands grab hold of her and thinks that's what a father must be like, with a strong grip like that.

'You're right, Bill! It's fine for any age. There you go, she's for you.'

He hands her the doll. She notices the milky skin, the shiny blonde hair sprouting from the porcelain scalp. She already knows how she is going to style it.

'What are you going to call this one?'

'Lila!'

'Lila?'

She sees her mother eyeing her strangely. So she reiterates: 'I'm going to call her Lila.'

'It's perfect! It's true the doll does look like your friend,' says Uncle Henri, a little awkwardly.

Louise rolls her eyes. She probably thinks it is a stupid choice of name, especially now that Lila has a shaved head.

'Are you Louise Savy's daughter?'

No one recognises her at Les Oliviers. It's not surprising – she has only ever visited once, and that was a long time ago.

'Sorry for your loss, madam. I'll take you to her room.'

'Thank you. I'll follow you.'

Billie listens to the sound her soles make on the old linoleum. It is familiar, the same sound over and over: that of a sticking plaster being ripped off. She takes in the plump figure of the manager as she leads the way. On hearing her voice on the telephone, Billie had immediately imagined a tall woman, lean and severe, but seeing her permed hair and smart suit, it strikes her that it is in fact possible to be happy at Les Oliviers. Billie focuses her mind on this observation, which saves her having to look at the blue doors and the names displayed on them.

It seems to take them an age to get there. All she wants is to collect her mother's belongings and get out of there as quickly as possible. She does not want to have to explain herself, to respond to the questions she can read in the manager's eyes: *Why did you never come back? What kind of a daughter are you?*

They eventually stop at one of the doors. Louise's name has already been removed. The place must be in demand.

A quick glance is enough to tell her what kind of state the room has been left in. Nothing has been moved. It will take her no more than a quarter of an hour to gather everything up.

'As I told you on the telephone, we didn't notice anything unusual. Louise was calm. She went up to her room at about seven o'clock. However, when I consulted the visitor log book,

I . . . I noticed that she'd had a visitor. I thought I ought to tell you. You know, your mother had so few visitors.'

Billie has the distinct impression the manager laid extra stress on those last words. And she frowned, too – barely perceptibly, but just enough to make Billie cast her eyes down.

'A man came to see her in the early afternoon.'

'A man? Do you know who it was?'

'I wasn't here. But Marilyn, one of our nurses, saw him. He went into your mother's room and came out again almost immediately.'

Billie turns to face the wardrobe, pretends to be gauging the amount of stuff. She memorises the name Marilyn. First she lifts down the items stored up high: the shoebox, a blanket, some jumpers that are not at all in the style of the Louise she had known. Then she moves on to the hanging space, takes the handful of skirts off their hangers. They are too long. Much too long. The skirts of a nun.

'It does happen sometimes, you know . . . When people aren't prepared. It's terrible for the family. For the nearest and dearest . . . Perhaps the man wasn't aware of your mother's state . . .'

Billie walks over to the bathroom and puts the toothbrush, a bar of soap and a tube of cream in a bag. She places her meagre collection on the bed and tries to dispel the memory of the drawers in V stuffed to overflowing with eyeshadows in every possible shade, eau de toilette bottles and ribbons in a rainbow of colours.

'Memory is a strange thing,' the manager goes on. 'It can happen that certain memories resurface completely out of the blue after years of total oblivion. We had a man who hadn't recognised his daughter for years who suddenly called her on her birthday. Some of the patients cry when they get these fleeting recollections. They suddenly become aware of their predicament and burst into tears.'

The drawer of the bedside table still needs emptying. Inside, Billie finds Louise's hairbrush. Before slipping it into her bag she touches the hairs caught in the bristles and has to fight back tears. There is something else at the back of the drawer. She pulls out a prayer book and glances, incredulous, at the manager.

'Hang on – I don't think this belonged to my mother.'

'Everything in here belonged to her.'

Billie reads the surprise in the manager's eyes. She is clearly not used to anyone disagreeing with her.

'It's impossible. She never used to—'

'Trust me. I assure you it was hers. Louise did pray some days, you know.'

'You must be mistaken. My mother—'

'I saw her praying on several occasions. She told me she was praying for . . . for the soldier.'

'I beg your pardon?'

She doesn't know whether it's the manager's sidelong glance or the incongruity of her words, but Billie feels she will explode if she doesn't get out of this room soon.

'Yes, those were her words. A soldier. Of course, you can't necessarily give much credence to what she said, given the circumstances, but I can tell you that those prayers were said in the rare moments when she seemed to be present.'

Billie scoops up all the things in her arms. The box, the clothes, the bag of rubbish and the prayer book.

'I think I've got everything.'

'I'll show you the way back.'

'Thank you, but there's no need. I know the way.'

Billie leaves the room, her arms full. She focuses again on the sound her shoes make on the linoleum. What's torn from you when you enter this place is not a plaster, but something much deeper.

She passes a nurse who glances at her as she goes by. She reads the name on the badge pinned to her uniform. Marilyn. It strikes her as odd, a name like that, here. And then she does an about-turn.

'Excuse me! I'm Billie, Louise Savy's daughter.'

'Oh, I'm sorry, madam. My condole—'

'I'm told that a man came to see her.'

'Yes, that's right. It was the day your mother—'

'Can you tell me more? I need to know whether the man spoke with her.'

No sooner has she uttered the question than she realises the stupidity of it: no one would have been able to talk with Louise.

'Well, he didn't stay long. It was around two in the afternoon if my memory serves me well. I saw him go into the room and come out again almost immediately. He was white as a sheet and—'

'I have an important question to ask you.'

'Yes?'

The young nurse pays attention, blushes slightly.

'Did he have red hair?'

'Girls! Where do you think you're off to like that?' Lila's mother calls.

'To the river!'

'Haven't you forgotten something?'

'Oh! Thank you, Suzanne!' Billie replies, scooping up the asthma inhaler.

Their footsteps echo down the little streets as they hurry along, kicking up dust with their sandals. Billie has one friend. A single friend, the one she has chosen out of all the girls in her school. Lila is the only one allowed to enter her world. Before Lila, her world was an impenetrable bubble. With Lila her world is still closed off, but it is inhabited by them both now. It is their own private world, the two of them thick as thieves from morning till night.

No one understands, of course. No one knows about the supernatural power that binds them one to the other, the life-blood of their sisterhood.

Billie once saw a programme about Siamese twin sisters who remained attached to one another for life. With Lila it is the same: they are touching, intertwined, two in one. Their hair mingles, the bushy with the straight, and they are linked at the arm. Inseparable.

Billie's tanned, scratched legs, her athletic build. Lila's hair blonde as wheat, her skin so pure. Her erratic breathing. Asthma attacks can come on at any moment, they had been told. They set off, armed with the inhaler. They trust each other completely. Absolutely. Billie knows exactly what to do. When she notices Lila's breath making a rasping noise in her throat, she takes the puffer and hands it to Lila, watching as she inhales through the mouthpiece.

They have reached the river and discarded their dresses and sandals. They make their way across the pebbles and the carpet of slippery moss. Uncle Henri is there, lounging in the water a little further along where it is shallow, his body an interface between the freezing river and the burning sun. With his face tilted upwards, angled toward the powerful heat source, he looks almost reptilian. Billie imagines he is charging himself up with solar energy before beginning his descent into deep water. His face is so white beneath the glare of the sun that he looks like a corpse. His ginger hair dances in the currents, one of its strands brushing intermittently against the rocks, like a shutter flapping open. Billie laughs at the sight of his skin, red in places, almost matching the intense glow of his incredible hair. He is turning into a lobster. She runs off to join Lila.

She can see Lila's swimsuit-clad bottom sticking out from under a flat rock, from which water is cascading down. The top half of her body is completely hidden beneath the rocky ledge. Billie crawls up next to her. 'Li-la!' 'Li-i-la!' It is Billie who calls out first. 'Bi-i-llie!' the other voice replies. Their shouts resound around the chamber formed by the curtain of water. They pause for a few seconds to listen to the echo that bounces back off the rock face. Their words remain imprisoned behind the din of the waterfall, their secrets secure.

'Are you hungry, girls?'

Uncle Henri has emerged from the water and is making his way awkwardly towards them. They pounce on the biscuits he has brought.

All three of them are sitting on a towel and Billie points at Lila's hair, which is plastered down towards the front of her head. The force of the water on the back of her head has practically gelled it down. This crown of hair on her head makes her look like one of those figures in the paintings on the wall of the village church; they have a similar yellow halo gracing their foreheads. Uncle Henri says they are saints.

Lila with her halo is a rather dishevelled saint. Her plaits have come undone; the hairbands that held them together have slipped out in the water.

Billie loves Lila's pale plaits; they could almost be straw. They are rough to the touch, flying outwards when she turns her head. Billie would like to have plaits like that.

But Lila thinks they are too fine. She is envious of Billie's crazy brown mass, her electric hair, which she helps her detangle after they have been swimming in the river. She has to tug at it, and ends up with loose hairs all over her hands.

'Shall we swap?'

They had been so excited at the idea.

2

The smells.

The potent smells of the house in V.

The searing heat of the summer and the stuffiness of the enclosed rooms in winter would combine to produce a sickening brew of mothball and lavender odours. These smells alone said much about V: closed cupboards filled with shabby clothes, stale air in the cramped bedrooms where draughts could never penetrate, heady scents compounded by sweat.

She remembered the sounds as well: the flies tap-tapping against the closed windows, the gasps in the night, the rustling of the sheets, the click of high heels going down the stairs before fading out of earshot, while her little fingers reached out, searched in the blackness for something or someone . . . Her tiny hand would touch the door through which her mother had disappeared. When would she be back? During the night, while she was sleeping? Perhaps one day she wouldn't come back.

Billie is now standing in the alley, facing the house. She takes in its stone walls, its red shutters, peeling and dusty, narrower than she remembered. The façade seems to have shrunk over the years. Even the old oak front door seems less imposing than it used to. All the same she feels incapable of walking those last few metres to go and open it.

She left it two days before coming here. After the funeral and the trip to Les Oliviers and back, she called on the solicitor. She also took the opportunity to arrange a meeting at the house, in a little while, with an estate agent. Had it not been for that appointment, she might not have mustered the courage to come back here.

Looking at the house, she thinks back to the solicitor's words. 'It seems Louise had a benefactor,' he had said, his nasal voice betraying a hint of curiosity. Billie had almost forgotten about that – the way people living in small communities are obsessed with wanting to know everything: how their neighbours live, who they are sleeping with, whether they are genuinely respectable or are hiding all kinds of guilty secrets . . . Louise must have been a perfect specimen for them: this girl who seemed as free as a bird, who was she really?

Billie made no comment when he explained that when Louise moved into Les Oliviers, she had not needed to sell the house to pay for her care. *It seems she had a benefactor.*

She listened to him distractedly, her mind preoccupied with what she would shortly have to do, namely go to the house and step inside.

They shook hands and Billie left with a single thought in mind: to find an estate agent and sell the house as quickly as possible. To wash her hands of the place where she had grown up.

She steps forward and finally enters the house. The smell hits her. It takes a moment for her eyes to adjust to the darkness. A few rays of light filter through the warped shutters. Little by little the old fireplace and the few items of furniture covered in dust-sheets emerge from the gloom, like living beings.

Everything was cleared when Louise left. Not a single object, vase or trinket remains.

She opens one of the windows and folds back the shutters to let the light in. That will do; she isn't planning on staying here long.

Holding the belongings brought back from Les Oliviers clamped to her front, she makes her way slowly up the stairs to the first floor, to their two bedrooms, separated by the narrow, low-ceilinged corridor. She stops, full of trepidation, outside what had been Louise's bedroom.

★ ★ ★

Tap tap. Tap tap.

Downstairs, her mother and Henri were sitting facing one another on the sofa, engrossed in their reading. Louise's foot was stroking Henri's thigh as he leafed through his newspaper. He made a point of buying one every morning – it was entertaining, he said. Billie didn't really understand what he meant by that. Sometimes he would read out an article to them: a flea market in a neighbouring village, an exhibition of paintings, a man attacked by a boar, a pétanque tournament.

Tap tap. Tap tap.

'Bill! Stop that!' Why is Louise still calling her that? She ought to know by now that it will just annoy her and that it won't stop her banging on the floor.

Tap tap.

'Bill!' When Louise is angry, her voice goes up a notch, becoming high-pitched and ugly. It seems to project straight out of her throat rather than rising gently from her stomach. It has a tendency to come unhinged on the last syllables.

Tap tap. Tap tap.

'It gets right on my nerves when she does that!' Billie hears her mother stand up, slip on her sandals and head up the stairs. The soles of her flip-flops slap against the steps.

Tap tap.

Voices are raised and Billie gives in. The footsteps go back downstairs. Louise flops down next to Henri and returns to her magazine. Billie and Lila sit down at the top of the stairs and dangle their legs between the bars.

'What was she doing?' Henri asks.

Louise sighs.

'It doesn't matter what she was doing.'

Billie and Lila carry on swinging their legs in mid-air in time with the ticking of the clock on the wall behind their heads.

'Come on, Lila, I want to show you something. But don't tell anyone! It's our secret. Okay?'

She fixes her friend with a very serious look. She is waiting for her go-ahead, her promise.

'What will be a secret, Billie?'

'You have to promise first!'

'It's hard to promise without knowing. Give me a clue!'

'Hold on, let me have a think.'

She draws a circle in the air with her index finger.

'What is it?'

'It's a hiding place. No one has ever found it.'

'We'll be the only ones to know about it?'

'Yes. If I show you, we'll be the only ones.'

She looks at her, bright-eyed.

Louise has gone upstairs to lie down in her room and has fallen asleep. The heat has taken it out of her. Billie pokes her head through the crack of the door and quickly registers Louise's face nestled in the hollow of the patterned pillow, her head seemingly encircled by a field of flowers. Silently she closes the bedroom door and calls to Lila. 'Come on, let's go!'

They have been walking for an hour. They grabbed a hunk of bread, a couple of slices of ham and a bottle of water on their way out, then Billie put everything in her rucksack and off they went, heading out of the village and joining the path that goes down to the river.

Billie keeps on going, leading Lila still further afield. She can already hear Lila's panting behind her. They stop for a rest and make short work of their sandwiches. Two red suns are blazing on Lila's cheeks. She passes her hands over her face, removes a stone from her sandal. Billie disappears briefly behind a thicket, then beckons her over. There is a hidden path leading into the forest.

Lila seems to hesitate at first, before following in her footsteps. She needs Billie to guide her here. Without her she would surely get lost.

'It's there, behind that curtain of leaves. Hold on, there's a password. You have to remember it.'

She invites Lila into her kingdom. She brings her lips to Lila's ear, beneath her blonde plait, and whispers the secret word.

'Did you hear it?'

Lila repeats it. She is hopping with impatience.

Then Billie sweeps aside the curtain of leaves. A little further along, on the right, hidden from view, there is a cave large enough to creep inside.

They sit down cross-legged on the damp ground, facing one another, and Billie produces a tin from her rucksack. Lila recognises it; it's the one where the biscuits are kept that they are always snacking on, leaving crumbs around the house. Billie likes the feel of the crunching under her bare feet in the morning. Those crumbs get everywhere.

Billie has placed the tin on her knees. She looks at the little smiling lady in traditional Alsatian dress on the lid. Lila probably thinks she is about to pass her a biscuit, but the items she takes out are much more intriguing: a torch, some string, some paper and pencils.

'We're going on an expedition!' she announces.

She has already stood up and is waiting for Lila.

They set off and Lila notices the pinkish walls covered in water droplets that glisten in the beam of the torch.

'Billie? Can you hear me?'

She hears Lila's voice faintly, muffled by the labyrinth of rocks. They have slipped through into a narrow corridor, a cave within a cave. They have barely gone any distance before Billie hears Lila whimpering and complaining of claustro-something-or-other. Such a chicken! So Billie quickens her step, leaving Lila to fend for herself. She will have to get used to the dark. Anyway, she will be able to see Billie's torch bobbing along ahead of her.

But Lila cannot go on. Behind Billie, the sound of breathing fades into the distance and disappears, swallowed up in the darkness. Lila is left blinded and bumping into the wet walls. The ground may have crumbled away in places, thinks Billie. Without a light to guide her, Lila could get sucked into a bottomless hole. She would disappear and no one would ever find her. Billie wouldn't even hear her cry of surprise the moment she falls. She would simply vanish into thin air. The tunnel of rock would swallow her whole and Billie wouldn't realise she was missing until long afterwards, when she returned to the place where she thinks she last saw her.

'Bill-i-ie!'

Now she can hear Lila stomping furiously, and it's pointless – all she's doing is going round in circles and grazing herself. She's panicking and her breathing has become hoarse and ragged. It sounds, in the pitch black, as though her breath is trapped inside her.

Billie knows she has to turn back. Lila jumps when Billie's hand touches hers in the darkness.

'All right? My torch went out. Come on. Let's go home.'

Tap tap!

No, it isn't little Bill's feet tapping on the floor tiles. No, she isn't dancing in the empty house. It is a different sound. A tentative sound at first, which then grows louder. Downstairs, someone is knocking at the door. Billie looks at her watch. The estate agent must be early. She is about to go back downstairs when she hears the voice above the knocks.

'Is anybody there?'

That voice . . . She freezes. Her hand grabs the banister.

'Billie? Are you there?'

One of the living room shutters is open; anyone pressing their face to the window would be able to spot her. So Billie stands motionless at the top of the stairs; she doesn't want to give herself away by moving at just the wrong moment.

'Is there anyone there?'

She is so persistent! Suzanne is going to end up attracting the neighbours' attention if she carries on with her racket. Doors will open, people will ask if they can help, the rumour mill will start turning and she will be trapped here. Cornered.

They don't know she is here. She took care not to pass anyone in V. You have to keep your wits about you in these insular communities where nothing goes unnoticed. Only the estate agent is aware. Presumably Suzanne will give up and go away at some point.

Billie sits down on the top stair and leans against the banister, running her hand over the worn wood. She used to lie down there, as a child, on the cool tiles, her legs dangling between the bars, listening to the sounds inside the house, the voices from downstairs. Right now, apart from Suzanne's shouts, the silence is dense. Inhabited by whispers, echoes, sighs. The house feels crowded. As if each of them had left something behind. She shivers and rubs her arms, turning over in her mind what she learned at Les Oliviers.

Her mother had so few visitors, as the manager had been at pains to point out. Suzanne probably came, unless the bonds between them had weakened over time. There may also have been one or two other visitors from V. But the man, the one who came to visit on the day she died, Marilyn had never seen him before. So that was the first time he had seen Louise again.

He had wanted to see her after all that time, but what might he have said or done to spark in her the desire to escape from her room in the middle of the night, trek all the way across the grounds, climb over the fence and go and throw herself in the water?

That is what's bothering her: after years of nothing, this man reappears in her mother's life and that very evening she drowns herself.

It is morning. Louise is in the kitchen with Suzanne, who has come to visit.

When Uncle Henri emerges from the bathroom, washed and shaven, the women are deep in conversation. Billie is busy with her colouring, but one ear is listening to everything they are saying. She always wants to know everything, understand everything. She also remembers everything. Now Louise and Suzanne seem to be talking about some kind of ultimatum.

'Yes, it's true!' Suzanne insists. 'She told him she would marry him provided he came to live with her on the coast.'

'What? But they seemed so—'

'Well, what d'you expect! She's a city girl, Louise! A proper townie with a shopping habit, a home hairstylist, a trouser suit, the lot. You really think she would give that all up? Although . . . for his beautiful eyes . . .'

'You're talking about beautiful eyes? Am I interrupting?'

'Henri!'

Suzanne plants a generous kiss on his cheek. She has left a red mark on his skin, which smears when he wipes it with the back of his hand. That's why Billie doesn't like kissing Lila's mother. She always wears such dark lipstick and that black crud on her eyelashes. She reminds her of a clown. They resume their conversation while Henri makes coffee.

Suzanne sucks so hard on the end of her cigarette that her cheeks go hollow. Billie's gaze stays riveted on her scarlet lips. Suzanne releases her nostrils, which had been pinched in with the effort, and puffs a cloud of smoke up towards the ceiling.

'My little Lila is becoming more and more secretive!'

'Oh, you have to let them grow up,' says Louise. 'They can't be tied to their mothers' apron strings for ever!'

'You're right, Lulu. I'm a proper mother hen!'

Suzanne turns around to face Henri.

'Ah, a coffee! Come here, my saviour!'

She takes the cup that Henri is holding out to her as if he were about to take it back again. She hoists herself onto the work surface, shuffling her bottom to get comfortable. From where she is sitting, Billie has a perfect view of Suzanne's slightly flabby thighs. Suzanne throws her head back when she laughs. Her head rolls around in a big circle, then her mouth opens, becomes enormous. She has yellow teeth.

Billie does like Suzanne, even if she does talk in a loud voice, has a funny way of doing her make-up and is always keeping tabs on Lila, unlike Louise, who doesn't really pay much attention to what Billie does. Lila's house is small and colourful, like a doll's house. Clean and tidy, not like hers. It is on two floors, with the bedrooms upstairs. Lila's parents have converted the loft into a bedroom for the baby brother they are hoping for. But for now there is no sign of him. Lila says that's why her mother cries sometimes and why she is always fussing over her, as you would a doll or a puppy.

The windows open onto the garden. The living room is filled with light, much more so than Billie's living room. It is almost dazzling when you get up in the morning and come down for breakfast. Lila and Billie, still in their nighties, skip out into the garden. The table is shaded by a parasol. This is Louise and Suzanne's place of refuge during the scorching summer months.

'Look!'

Both of them have stepped out from under the parasol and are using their hands to shade their eyes. They are hoping to catch a glimpse of the fire-fighting plane, a shadow passing across the blinding sphere of the sun.

'Lila, come and see the plane, my darling! Lila! Come and look!'

Suzanne is bubbling with excitement.

'Oh leave her be, Suzie! She's seen thousands of fire-fighting planes!'

Lila's father winks at Henri. Billie hears him whisper something.

'It's the same drama every summer!'

Every year forest fires break out, fanned by the winds. They wipe out everything in their path. The hills remain bare, grey with dust and ashes, for years afterwards, until in the end the vegetation grows back.

Above their heads, the sky is filled with the drone of engines and the great metal birds perform their sombre dance.

The garden is huge. Suzanne may complain that there isn't enough space for a swimming pool, but for Billie and Lila it's a paradise. It has bushes around the edge that prevent the neighbours from seeing in, and the girls have a place hidden from view where they can spy on any goings-on outside the house. Louise and Suzanne often lie there on sunbeds talking and smoking. At the very end of the garden, up against the fence, is a wooden shed where Lila's father keeps his tools. The girls have nailed bits of fabric to the walls to cover up the holes in the planks. The shed leans slightly to one side, but it's their den. Their palace.

'They spend hours in there! I'd like to know what they get up to!' Lila's father's words send the girls into fits of laughter.

They watch everything from here, notice everything, know everything. It was from here that they heard Suzanne talking about the little brother who hasn't materialised. It was here, too, that Billie heard her mother whispering that she was too young, that it had been too soon for her. Billie did not really understand what she meant by that, but she felt a lump form in her throat. Afterwards, Louise talked about Uncle Henri. She said it was too late, that he had a family elsewhere. Billie knew what that *elsewhere* referred to: Henri's native region, the place where the dolls he gave her each year came from.

It was there, also, that the idea of a swap came to them, the summer when they were ten. Originally Lila had wanted to use her father's razor, but Billie thought it would be better to do it with scissors – they were more accurate and cut better. They had to get it right, because if they messed up, it would probably take an age to grow back! So they practised on Billie's dolls. Uncle Henri had brought her so many.

Billie had gone first with the scissors. She had carefully brought the blades up close, poking her tongue out as she did so, and laid them flat against the porcelain head, at the base of the hair. Lila had closed her eyes and prayed aloud: *Please make it work!*

'Do you agree, madam?

'Sorry?'

'Shall I draw up the contract?' the estate agent asks.

Billie acquiesces, happy with the way everything has gone: the tour of the house, the professional demeanour of the greying man in his fifties, his pertinent questions, his efficiency. He has played the game, has understood Billie's priorities: speed matters more than price. She can trust him to take things in hand and keep her updated. He didn't miss a trick, trying early on to persuade her to grant his agency an exclusive sales mandate. Not that it matters. In any case, she has no choice. She just wants to dispose of the house, clear it out, give the last remaining contents to charity or to anyone who wants them. There might be antiques enthusiasts interested in taking the furniture. 'Give it to them,' she told the agent, 'tell them they can have what they want from the house.' They must be period pieces. Nothing has changed here for centuries!

'You're going back to Paris?'

'Yes. I'm flying back tomorrow afternoon.'

'Have a good flight then.'

Billie closes the door. Silence envelops her again. She recoils slightly at the sight of the white sheets draped over the furniture, looking like ghosts standing stock-still. She is tempted to lift them off, to check that, underneath, everything is still intact. The yellowed floral pattern on one of the armchairs that she used to trace with her finger when she was drowsy. The old scratches on the wooden sideboard. The pedestal table where she used to leave her exercise books. It would be too much. She is already having to contend with the heady odour in the house, the silence thick with sighs, the old soot-blackened fireplace which seems to be beckoning her, waiting for her to light a fire there again.

She is about to go back upstairs when three brief knocks on the front door make her turn around. She swings the door open.

'Have you forgotten some—?'

The man stands there wide-eyed, resting his indulgent gaze on her just as he did when she was little.

PART THREE
Louise

I

He is here, in front of her. He looks her in the eye, self-consciously. He tells her he is sorry. *Sorry, Billie. My condolences.*

The years have left their mark, but his gaze is unchanged. His eyes can still read her: her astonishment, her silence deep as the sea, her anger.

'Come in. No need to stay on the doorstep.'

She opens the door to this man who has walked straight out of her childhood, shows him into the living room – forgetting for a moment how well he knows this house – and pops into the kitchen. 'I won't be long!' She searches the empty cupboards, delaying the encounter. She manages to unearth two glasses.

He is sitting on the sofa draped in its white sheet, facing the window. He seems to be watching the motes of dust dancing in the shaft of light. Before going over to join him, Billie takes in the curve of his back, his still muscular arms resting on his bony knees, his hands covered with sun spots, the wrinkled skin on the nape of his neck. She tries to remember, to retrieve an image resembling this one, but none comes to mind. When he used to sit in that same place, next to Louise, she would sometimes sneak up behind him and wrap her little arms around his neck. Or perhaps her memory is playing tricks on her. What was his skin like, back then? Did it have that same greyish tinge? The very sight of Henri here, back in the house in V, is warping her memories, superimposing itself on them like tracing paper.

He has heard her come in and straightens up. His presence seems so natural, on this sunny late afternoon.

'Bill!'

She winces at the dropped syllable.

'I don't have much to offer you . . . As you can see, the house is bare.'

She places the two glasses and her bottle of mineral water on the coffee table in front of them. They sit side by side like two awkward kids, embarrassed by the closeness of their bodies but determined not to move apart.

'I wanted to see her again, Billie. I tracked her down to that place . . .'

'Les Oliviers.'

'Yes, that's it, Les Oliviers. She didn't recognise me.'

'I know.'

Billie can picture their failed reunion, the gaping void in Louise's eyes when the stranger enters her room, approaches her and pleads with her in words she does not understand. Lulu. My Lulu.

'Billie. You look—'

The words are trapped in the air between them.

'You look radiant.'

They eye each other like two vultures as Henri lights a cigarette, takes a drag, savours it. He seems to be clinging to it like a life raft.

'Where do you live, Billie?'

'In Paris.'

'Whereabouts in Paris?'

'In the twentieth arrondissement.'

'Oh. Right.'

He is studying the movements of the water in his glass with interest.

'You know the twentieth arrondissement?'

'A bit – not very well, to be honest . . . How long have you been living in Paris?'

'For quite a few years.'

'Quite a few years . . .'

He seems to be weighing this information, as if it could shed light on everything else.

'And what do you do in Paris?'

'Are you going to quiz me on everything, Henri? And why have you actually come here?'

'Billie! Stop it, please.'

His anger has flared so abruptly that it almost takes her by surprise. Her gaze travels over the familiar face. The freckles around the nose, the red hair that used to fascinate her. The shoulders, which, from her low vantage point as a child, looked so solidly built, seem to have shrunk. They appear quite small seen from here. She wonders whether it is an optical illusion, whether her own perceptions are distorted and whether any comparison with the Henri of days gone by has become impossible today, now that she has the body of a woman.

She would have liked him to look her bravely in the eye and give her all the explanations she has never had. Instead, she sits facing downcast eyes.

'Did you think about her, *Un-cle* Henri?'

She separates each syllable.

'Don't call me that, Billie.'

'Have I ever called you anything else?'

'It was complicated, Billie. Complicated, you see . . .'

'But what about now? Why? Why did you come and see her after all this time? What were you after, Henri? What were you hoping to find in that place?'

Billie notices she has raised her voice.

'What—'

He stares at her, nervously stubs out his cigarette.

'You turn up at Les Oliviers after . . . how many years? Ten? Fifteen? And on that very same evening, she . . . she's found drowned.'

'What are you insinuating, Billie?'

She sees how his eyes widen, his lip trembles. She is momentarily calmed by that trembling lip.

Then Henri smiles at her – with that modest smile she knows

so well – and it is as if the endless path she has been travelling since childhood has melted away. What age is she now? Six years old again, like the first time she met him? They say time changes people. You might run into someone on a street corner one day, and not recognise them at first. It takes you a while to remember a name, to make the connection to a certain period in your life, because of all those minute changes in the body, in the voice, that add up and turn the person into a stranger.

But the others, the exceptional few – the people you have loved – they never seem to leave you. Henri is there, right next to her, and nothing has changed between them. He talks to her in that serious, enveloping voice that so moved her as a child: with him around, she noticed how she was treated as someone to be cuddled and protected.

'I'm trying to understand . . . I'm trying to understand what could have happened in Louise's head to make her do that.'

'I don't know, Billie. The fact is she didn't see me. There was no one in that blasted room. I tried to talk to her. I wanted to bring her back. Just for a moment. But it wasn't her. It wasn't Louise.'

He sighs, pulls out another cigarette.

'As for why I came looking after all this time . . . How shall I put it? You know how a magnet repels and attracts? It was like that with Louise and me.'

2

'I've never known anything like it! It's murder! Henri, love, watch out for the sun, it's hotter than it looks.'

'Yes, Mum!'

Summer 1960. Henri's parents had rented the house with the green shutters on the outskirts of the village, their first time. It was a two-storeyed building overlooking a garden with just enough space for a swimming pool and a small patio.

The hinterland was paralysed by a general torpor at the time, its inhabitants on edge beneath a stormy sky.

It was that summer that Henri met Louise. A summer of limp bodies, of siestas by the pool. The chlorine seeping between their lips when they dived into the warm water, Louise swimming over to him with broad strokes, a metre of water beneath their feet and the hum of wasps above their heads. Stretched out on the grass, panting, water trickling from their swimming costumes, they allowed their bodies to be permeated by the heat of the raging furnace. Louise watched, intrigued, as an ant made its way over Henri's delicate skin. While her skin naturally soaked up the sun, his would burn.

They were sixteen. They were free. Those could be the opening words of Henri's story: the story of a holiday romance.

That summer, like every summer, there had been a dance. It was the highlight of the season, a get-together for the people of V and the neighbouring villages. As it was a special occasion, Henri had been given permission to stay out until ten. He hung around in the square, alone, as the dance band played. It was his first summer here and he knew no one. On the far side of the square were some fairground rides, and this was where most of the young people from the village had gathered. A few elderly people had ventured into the middle of the dance floor and were shakily attempting a kind of tango. Amused, Henri had watched them for a while until he had had enough. He been about to stroll over to the fairground stalls when he noticed her.

She was standing back from the dance floor, in the company of three other girls. They were pointing at someone on the dance floor and she had suddenly roared with laughter. And that rich, vibrant laugh had carried all the way over to him, sparking an explosion inside him. He couldn't have put into words what had brought on this shock, but he had sat down on the little wall bordering the square and from this perfect spot, where it looked as if he was watching the dancers, he had observed her. Brown-haired, not very tall, with red ballet pumps on her feet, she was wearing a gingham dress – he had heard his mother mention this fabric while browsing her beloved fashion magazines – that was fitted down to the waist, then flared extravagantly outwards all the way to her ankles, as if she had ten underskirts on underneath. Although the long skirt was old-fashioned for someone her age, it suited her. Anything, even the ugliest item of clothing, would have looked good on this remarkable girl. You could tell at a glance that the dress had been bought at a budget store or hand-sewn by fingers that, though able, were not exactly expert. She moved like a goddess in this quaint dress his grandmother might have worn, tossing her hair back in a slightly provocative manner, and again his heart skipped a beat when, for a split second, he was convinced she had met his gaze. Under the brazen eye of this would-be Bardot, he had quickly sat up straight, puffed up his skinny torso and passed a damp hand over his hair, greasy with traces of the sun cream his mother slathered all over him. *You need to watch out for your skin, my darling. The sun's vicious here!*

Then the girl had suddenly disappeared from his field of vision. He had stood up in a rush, cast an eye all around to see where she had gone, and soon spotted the gingham dress going along on the other side of the dancers. He had followed her from a distance, bumping into people who got in his way, as she seemed to just glide along in front of him. Hindered by the obstacles, he lost track of her. He retraced his footsteps in the hope of catching sight of her, but his search was in vain. He could only conclude that she had vanished into thin air.

The next day he gave the pool a miss and found various excuses to go and hang around in the village, but he did not see her again. In the early afternoon lull, the streets were deserted and everything was so brutally exposed under the blinding light – the peeling paint, the gathered dust – that the buildings them-selves seemed stricken with the heat. Only a handful of pétanque players, caps pulled down firmly on their heads, had ventured outside and were half-heartedly lobbing their balls. Meanwhile the youth of the village were nowhere to be seen. Where had they all gone? What did young people get up to during the midday heat of summer? Did they have their secret hangouts where they could set the world to rights, smoke, flirt? Alone and idle, his eyes scanning the place for the girl who had haunted his thoughts since the previous day, Henri would have dearly liked to know.

And then, after two days of hanging around, he finally spotted her. After dinner he had announced that he was going for a stroll to get some fresh air. The afternoon had been so oppres-sive that it felt as if a thunderstorm might erupt at any moment. Some of the fairground rides were still open and, as he approached, he immediately recognised her dishevelled hair that hung down to her waist, blown by the wind that was now stir-ring. She held her outstretched arms firmly in position, tensed just enough to ensure her aim would not waver at the moment of firing. Displayed above her head along the entire length of the shooting gallery were knick-knacks, big cuddly toys and dressing-up outfits. The rifle in her hands made her look tiny. Henri thought of her gingham dress. He could imagine her having won it there, the top prize. *A Brigitte Bardot dress for the young lady! Well done, miss!*

She fired her first shot, which was a good aim. The jolt sent her shoulder backwards. Then she adjusted her position. Apart from white ballet pumps, she was dressed all in pink, in a sleeveless blouse and a mid-calf-length skirt. Henri walked discreetly up behind her, fiddling with the coins in his pocket, and hung back as if he was waiting his turn. The man in charge of the stall gave him a nod and went over to the crate containing the other rifles. *Bang!* A second shot rang out, this one mingling with an unexpected, thunderous sound that made all three of them look up. A fork of lightning tore through the sky, which had suddenly darkened, a powerful gust of wind whipped up the stalls' tarpaulin covers and the newspapers and paper cups that were lying around. Then came the rain – big fat drops that soaked them in a matter of seconds, transforming the square into a giant paddling pool. Henri saw the pink skirt and white ballet pumps disappear behind the sheet of rain. He too ran for the nearest cover.

He squeezed under a porchway that was barely big enough to shelter him, and didn't immediately notice the figure huddled behind him in the recess. He jumped when she emerged from her shadowy corner, stepped forward with a sigh and came to stand next to him. They watched the spectacle of the elements unleashed over V, the forks of lightning streaking the sky, the fearsome rumbles of thunder that made the walls of the booths shake, suddenly taking their occupants hostage, trapping them under the canopies, but also bringing some welcome cool. They stood side by side, dazed and shivering, soaked from head to toe. Henri offered silent prayers of gratitude to the heavens as the storm raged on, leaving the two of them stranded together in this shelter, so cramped that, standing next to her, he could feel the heat radiating off her and catch the smell of her wet clothes. Her teeth were chattering. 'Hi!' she said, and he turned his gaze upon her blurry face. She must have been wearing make-up because she had black trickles running down her cheeks. One might have been forgiven for thinking she had been crying, but she laughed and declared: 'God must be angry this evening!' And it was this first image of Louise that he always remembered: this girl from the south, suntanned and dripping in her pink blouse, which was clinging to her skin, her nakedness beneath the transparent fabric making her blush.

That first summer, Henri fell in love not only with her but also with every facet of her world: Louise *was* the south – the scents, the sounds, the music and the whole buzz of it – the whistling wind, the chirping crickets, the dizzy dance of the bumblebees . . . She was its changing light, its myriad hues, mimosa and oleander, the purple carpets of the lavender fields, brittle golden grass, buckwheat, scents of rosemary, thyme and savory. She was the quivering of the hot air, the crumbs of earth trapped in your sandals, the squelching of bare feet in wet flip-flops, tired bodies roaming the steep hillsides, hands plucking blackberries and wild strawberries along the way, grey wagtails all year round, hornets buzzing above feverish foreheads, before the thunderstorms came and swept the heat away. She knew all the creatures that inhabited this landscape: birds, dragonflies, butterflies, grass snakes and creepy crawlies. Like her they were born and lived their lives here, confined to this territory with boundaries visible to them alone, boundaries that kept them here as if this were the only place capable of supplying their needs. A trap.

As changeable as the seasons, the sunny Louise was often eclipsed by the other Louise, the sullen one. Eccentric, selfish, headstrong, exasperating. Are you sulking? He was sorely tempted to give her a good shake sometimes, but he held back, for Louise's fits of temper amounted to more than just sulking. She had mood swings, and would flee from his arms, later returning more obsessed than ever, as if in the wake of a storm.

He hated that Louise. Seized by a kind of stunned ecstasy, mute before this girl with the brittle heart, he allowed his young and inexperienced self to be pushed around. He would have gladly shaken some sense into her had he not been the well-brought-up young man he was. But then the sun would come out again. She would call him back to her with a gesture of infinite tenderness, an about-turn that left him transfixed with

happiness. And he rediscovered her body. That perfect body. The
first body he had known.

Under her hair, which she rarely wore up, she had a nasty scar
running along the base of her neck – it would later be joined by
the other one, on her wrist. The pinkish mark would swell, shrink
or turn purple depending on the day or the ambient temperature.
On her moods, maybe. How did that happen? He wanted to ask
her that simple question, but he sensed, from the moment he
discovered it, that the story it concealed would stay where it was:
buried under her swollen skin.

   While Louise is sleeping on a flat rock, he lifts the damp
tendrils of her hair, gently touches the scar, leans forward and
kisses it. He lies down again, troubled. Still a little out of breath
from their bracing swim, he listens to Louise's regular breathing,
barely audible over the tumult of the river flowing past down
below, a sound so incessant and deafening that he feels a kind
of intoxication come over him.

'This is going to sound crazy to you, Billie, but that scar haunted
me, whispered things to me. She thought it was vile, but for me
it was an anchor. I cherished that flaw on her body because it
made her human in my eyes.'

   'That's a nice story, Henri, but you're forgetting one thing:
Louise never went to the river; she hated it there.'

   'No, Billie. Not when I met her. On the contrary, you couldn't
tear her away from it. She was just like you, there from dawn till
dusk. It was years later that she stopped going there . . .'

   'Whatever! That's just a minor detail, isn't it?'

   Billie grabs the bottle of water, fills her glass, but does not
drink from it. Discovering this other Louise makes her nervous.
How could they have lived side by side and been oblivious to so
many things about each other?

A year passes. Henri returns to V the following summer, then
the ones after that. His parents always rent the house with the

green shutters. He and Louise spend three more summers together, languishing under the piercing light. Three summers that will become an obsession for him. And against this static backdrop, they grow up, they change. Henri watches Louise's parents, Adele and Jacques, at mass every Sunday.

'Pious Adele . . . You look so much like her, Billie. You have her eyes. I barely knew her, our paths only crossed once or twice, but I remember the colour of them. I'd never seen eyes like hers before. And yours are the same. Eyes like honey . . .'

Louise's parents are there every Sunday. They pray, their faces serious. Adele takes communion, paying little attention to the skinny red-head who greets her timidly. Her mind is focused on other things. But Henri will have plenty of time to get to know them because he knows he will be back each summer, year after year, until the day he leaves there once and for all, with Louise. He will take her away from V, take her wherever she longs to go. They will find a place of their own somewhere, he already knows, for their love is eternal, like the river current. It will never change.

Then came that day. 25 August. The date is etched in his memory. His attempts to banish it are in vain; it has remained lodged somewhere inside him.

It is late on that 25 August, but it is still daylight. The sky is pure, heralding a clear night. Henri goes to meet Louise at the main square as arranged. She is sitting on the little wall bordering the square and watching the last of the summer festivities. He knows that the holiday season is drawing to a close, that soon he will have to return to his part of the world, to the north but, more than that, it is the sight of Louise's poker-straight back that brings a lump to his throat. That way she has of sitting there, saying nothing. He walks up to her and enfolds her in his arms.

Beneath her sun-bronzed shoulders, all her muscles are tense. Louise's body is a spring stretched to its limit. She has withdrawn into herself and her silence is worse, much worse, than any words she might throw in his face. He would prefer that. Words.

He straightens up, stays standing behind her. He cannot sit down next to her; she has drawn a clean dividing line between them. She's no longer there; he can feel it. She has dissolved, retreated from the scene of confrontation. He looks at her sitting down there in front of him, imprints her in his memory: her messy hair – the untidy parting, a single white hair in amongst all the brown. And yet she is so young. If only he could pull it out. It's a thick one. It shouldn't be there.

'Are you sulking, Lulu?' That edge to his voice. It's strange, the way his voice cracks without warning.

She looks up at him with an irritated expression, impatient for him to leave. In that split second he hates her. How quickly you can hate someone! A look is all it takes. The urge to insult, to hurt, to strangle, to curse, to make love again, to get on your knees and beg.

Louise's skin is flushed, a prominent vein running across her forehead. He hardly recognises her; this person is nothing like her. His Louise is capable of controlling herself, of exuding an Olympian calm, of being a touch arrogant some days. Phlegmatic.

'Why? Why?' he stammers miserably. What does he want her to reply? That this wasn't planned? That love is not fixed, that it can be changeable, or that it can run out of steam?

'Say something, for goodness' sake!'

His voice is imprisoned in his throat. He can't utter a sound. He wishes he could hold her back, plead his case, but the words hop around inside him like hyperactive fleas. Louise stands up. She turns this way and that, making him feel dizzy. That's it, she is about to leave. He could pull out all the stops, assume the heartrending role of the abandoned lover. He gauges the distance between them, but already she is no more than a solitary figure moving rapidly away from him.

'I've often thought about the days leading up to that 25th of August. I went over and over them in my mind for any hints, signs. I wanted to understand . . . To understand what could have prompted Louise to break up with me so suddenly.'

If he had known, would he have been able to put things right? That question has haunted him. His nervous fingers slide out another cigarette.

'When I got back home, to Alsace, I wrote her a letter . . .'

He had shut himself in his bedroom and committed everything to paper, his love, his rage, the questions spinning around in his head. Then he had hurried to the post box in a frenzy.

'I didn't have the courage to send it. In any case, I don't think that letter would have changed anything. Louise's decision was final. And my words were . . . I don't know . . . the words of an immature, angry young man.'

Back in his room, out of breath, he had torn them up, those crude, ridiculous words. Louise would never get to see them. Just as she would never see his tears. He had thrown the torn shreds in the bin, hiding them at the bottom under the other rubbish. Those remnants of his anguished love. His shame.

'For a long time I waited for something to happen . . . Anything . . . Some radical change of circumstances that would make her come back. And then in the end I got over it. I forgot her.'

He had erased Louise from his mind in the same way one erases childhood fancies.

'But you came back all the same,' murmurs Billie.

'Yes, years later. I had to. I had no choice. How can I put it? It was something I needed to do. They say your first love can stay with you your whole life. I think that, in my case, my love was somehow bound up with V, as if that was the only place it could exist. Anywhere else it would have gone cold. I'm sure that if Louise and I had met somewhere else, our love would have withered.'

'Then you found us.'

'You were six years old, Billie. I had already built a life of my own. I could tell you that I was consumed by guilt, but that wouldn't be true. I felt a pressing need. I had to come back and, deep down, I was certain Louise would still be here. At the same time I knew she used to dream of a different life. She always said there was a glittering career awaiting her elsewhere. "I want to be an actress," she used to say. There are drama schools in Paris, prestigious ones. She seemed so confident. To be honest, I thought she was worryingly naive. But I would let her talk; I think deep down I enjoyed it. She was dead set on it: her big getaway, acting, success. And yet I still imagined, when I came back, that she would be waiting for me, even though she had rejected me without so much as a word of explanation. There was a little voice in my head spurring me on. Go on! You've got nothing to lose!'

Henri had got married. He had asked for the hand of a woman he was quite fond of, and they had found a house in a remote corner of Alsace, with a garden large enough for the whole family to take advantage of over the summer. When Henri married Anne, they had known each other a few months. In the early days he revelled in the peacefulness of his shared life with her. They got married in the church in the village they had just moved to. In her sculpted white dress, hugging her narrow waist, she smiled at him as she said *yes* and looked at him slightly dazed, as if she had just woken from a long nap.

Henri's career was heading in the right direction. They went on to have two boys, and Anne took care of them while also working part-time. They were a model family – the epitome of happiness, the envy of their neighbours – but Henri was suffocating. His life became a noose that was slowly squeezing the life out of him, until one May day he decided to get out of there, on the pretext of attending a training course.

The desire to return to V had lodged and deepened in him – ebbing at times, only to flow back stronger, like the tides. The call of the outside world, Louise would have said. Eventually he succumbed to the pull of the currents and set off for the place that had become an obsession with him, that gloomy house with its oppressive thick stone walls and stale smell of dust.

That old building *was* Louise. She and it were the same: melancholic, possessed of remarkable strength but exposed to all weathers, a combination of solid masses and empty spaces, liable to crumble at any moment. And beneath the fragrance of cheap perfume, Louise had her own indefinable, faintly sour odour, as if the stale smell of the house had gradually impregnated her skin. She was born there and would never live anywhere other than in that closeted space.

At the same time she talked constantly about getting out of there. She wanted to escape the deadly boredom. Perhaps she has left. Right now she is probably travelling the world. This thought goes round and round in Henri's head as he is driving to V on that day in May 1970, nearly seven years after their last summer together.

As he drives, his stomach clenched, his hands sweaty on the steering wheel, he thinks about what he's going to do when he arrives at the village. Get a room in the only hotel, open the window and listen to the sounds ringing out in the narrow alley; watch a lizard creeping along the wall, put on a pair of shorts and his espadrilles and track down the house with the green shutters. Listen to the murmur of the water in the swimming pool behind the wall encircling the property, stand on tiptoes and smell the chlorine. Feel the burning urge to push open the gate, enter the garden and dive into the pool, to the alarm of the swimmers who suddenly find their privacy so rudely invaded by this madman, then explain to them that he once lived in this house, that he has spent part of his childhood in this place and that he needs to know what life is like here without him. Apologise for disturbing them, then resume his journey under the sun that seems intent on sapping the life from him, cursing the fact his water bottle is empty.

That first evening back in V, showered and shaven, he had noticed the streets getting busier and the sound of a band playing. Nervously, he had run a comb through his hair, picked up his cigarettes and headed downstairs. He wove his way through the streets, following the sound of the music. On the square, paper lanterns swayed in the gentle breeze. It was the same square full of promise that he had known aged sixteen. Their square, his and Louise's.

He had mingled with the crowd of dancers, had drunk until his head was spinning. Already, past and present were starting to merge in his mind, but the sudden sight of a suntanned ankle attached to a foot in an espadrille had brought them into head-on collision. Wide-eyed, his gaze had travelled over the worn denim dungarees that clung tightly to her bottom, the mass of electric hair hanging down the full length of her back. All of a sudden he had been thrown off-balance, unsettled, just as he had been that summer when he was sixteen, by the dazzling sight of Louise, true to type in her old-fashioned dungarees, still here, doing her own thing, in this southern backwater.

All he had to do was go to the main square, the beating heart of V, and mingle with the night-time revellers. There would be no need to make a frantic search or question the neighbours. In the time it had taken him to discover that nothing had really changed apart from the odd minor detail – the bakery's new coat of paint, a newsagent's in the place where the hair and beauty salon used to be – Louise had appeared, an intrinsic part of the scenery. And at the sight of her he was neither the Henri of old nor the Henri of today, but felt himself to be in some confusing, indeterminate zone.

He felt the same buzz of excitement and energy as his sixteen-year-old self, a new, unexpected fervour propelling him into action. And the lies, the weight of them. He sat at the desk in his hotel room, poring things over. He wanted to write a few lines to Anne and the children, to let them know he was thinking of them. A simple letter to show that his absence was of no consequence, that the world order was unchanged. *I'm thinking of you. The training course is deadly boring and I'm missing you* . . . Ashamed, he ripped up the sheet of paper and started over again. After an hour, with a dozen balls of paper scattered at his feet, he gave up, opting for silence. And every year Anne welcomed him back in the same way when he returned from his training courses, suntanned and reinvigorated. She said nothing. Adopted the same approach as him – feigned ignorance – in order to avoid confrontation.

★ ★ ★

Billie knows that Henri has reached the crucial part of his story. She notices it in his voice, which has slowed down, and the changed pattern of his breathing, as night begins to fall.

'It was a few days after we got back together that disaster struck,' he says. He takes another cigarette. He cannot bring himself to look her in the eye – at least that is the impression she gets.

'I had walked Louise to her front door. We had arranged to meet up again a bit later. I wanted to take her to a restaurant by the sea. I was planning to go back to the hotel, have a shower and phone home.'

It was years ago and yet it was only yesterday . . .

Billie remembers: just as Henri is stepping away from Louise, he senses her presence next to them. He must have heard her sandals crunching on the gravel. He gives a start and turns round.

'Billie, it's you!' is all that Louise manages to stammer. In the dark alley Henri can dimly make out the indistinct shape of a little girl, her figure silhouetted against the light. Her boyish frame. The shock of hair cascading over her narrow shoulders. She has inherited her mother's crazy mane. Now, as she steps forward into the square patch of light, he notices the traces of dirt on her knees, the bits of twig caught up in her hair, the dried salt on her cheeks.

'Bill, go back inside please. Come on, don't stay there. Off you go!'

She had walked across in front of them, a fleeting figure. In that brief moment he had noticed her strange eyes, her pupils ringed with yellow. Like her grandmother Adele, she had cat's eyes dotted with glints of gold. And she had that lean body that had reminded him of the way he himself had looked as a child growing up in the north, swamped by his clothes and dreaming of being a man.

Henri had known even before his brain had done the calculation: the little girl he had just seen must be six years old. Seven at most. Go back seven years and you arrive at their last summer in the house with the green shutters.

★ ★ ★

'The rest you know, Billie . . .'

He stubs out his cigarette, looking for a sign of acknowledgement in her eyes.

'No, that's just it, I don't know the rest . . . I don't know the end and I don't know the beginning.'

She places a distinct emphasis on this last word. Because that is the source of the void, the silence that was a common thread throughout her childhood, like a cold, dry breath of air. In that dysfunctional family formed by the three of them – Bill, Louise and Henri – nothing was talked about, and it was this silence that enabled them to keep going. But today Billie is ready, she wants to hear all of it.

'Louise never wanted to talk about that particular summer . . . The summer when you were conceived . . . I pressed her, I wanted to know . . . To know the reasons for her silence, for her decision to distance herself from me. But you know what your mother was like – she dug her heels in, she wouldn't talk about it. Or hardly . . .'

Louise had not spoken about the unexpected burden she now had, about the reason for her evasiveness, her awkwardness. He had fathomed it out himself, just as he had suddenly understood the Louise of 25 August, seven years before – the one sitting on the little wall in the square, uncommunicative, wrapped up in her own fear. If only he had listened to her instead of harassing her. If only he had guessed . . . But can one ever guess such things?

'All she said to me was that . . . that she wasn't ready when it happened.'

Anger flares again in Billie's stomach.

I wasn't ready. Isn't that what Louise had said? *I wasn't ready.*

Of course she wasn't ready. She probably never had been. Louise was ready for all sorts of things, but not that. Not for a little human being utterly dependent on her. Greedy for her.

In all Billie's memories, Louise is absent. Even when she is with her, her mother is absent. She wants to be left in peace. Wants her little Bill to leave her in peace.

Her reluctant mother spends a long time doing her hair, applying oil to it, working it through with her fingers to tame the strands, something that Billie, with her wild-child looks, has never been able to do. Yet she has watched her on numerous occasions, sitting on the bed in the bedroom with the little balcony, her legs dangling in the air. Billie is six, eight, twelve, utterly absorbed in watching her mother do her hair. She studies her actions with the same concentration she devotes to her school-work. Louise herself smiles, her mind focused on something other than her own demons. She forgets her daughter is there.

'And Adele? And Jacques?' asks Billie.

Louise had told Henri about the accident that had occurred four years earlier: Adele at the wheel, the typical twisting roads of the region, the dazzle of the headlights in the night, the car lurching and rolling over.

'You must have been two when it happened. And Louise still so young.'

The shock of their disappearance, the panic, the sadness, the absence: she had never spoken of these things. Whenever he mentioned her parents, Louise became mute. It was as if she had obliterated them from her memory. She had even removed all evidence of them from the house. Nothing remained, not a photo, not a single souvenir of them. And in forgetting Adele and Jacques, Louise had also forgotten God. She had got rid of her rosaries, her prayer books and crucifixes, and at the same time had rejected the beliefs that had always been part of her life.

'Are you sure about that, Henri? I was under the impression that Louise used to pray . . .'

Billie thinks of the prayer book she found in the bedroom drawer at Les Oliviers, of the manager's assurances.

'I don't know, Bill. I never understood what it was that led her to make such a drastic decision. Adele was so pious . . . Louise grew up surrounded by religion. Perhaps it was a form of denial. Her way of dealing with the sudden death of her parents.'

★ ★ ★

She hadn't grown any calmer over time, of course. On his return to V, Henri had found both the sunny Louise and the sullen one. But he had also discovered another, more tormented one. Louise had changed. She was more unstable, gripped by obsessions. On some days she would hide herself away and seemed angry at the whole world. She was nervous in her movements, slammed doors, knocked over anything in her path. She would fume. And then, when you least expected it, she would return, re-enter everyday life. She was back. As if she had been away on a trip or out all night. And those who lived alongside her would emerge exhausted from the ordeal.

Ever since Henri had found her again, Louise had had nightmares. She would wake him up in the night, breathless, bathed in sweat, as if she had just been battling a wild animal. He would shake her until she surfaced from her dreams.

In the end he had grown used to her nightmares, to their recurring themes. It was always the same images that came up again and again.

'Terrible images, Billie. Images of war and death. She talked about an accident, a body in the river. Goodness knows where she got that from!'

Suddenly there is a film of sweat on Billie's forehead as Henri continues.

A body in the river . . . Did Louise know? Had she always known? Billie recalls her mother's expression that last summer in V, before she had run away with her entire life-savings in her pocket; recalls the way her mother had looked at her. Was it disgust? Was Louise looking at her with disgust?

No, of course not, Billie had got it wrong. The accident of that summer, her own accident, came quite a bit later. Lila and she were sixteen. Henri had been aware of Louise's nightmares for a long time before that. It was a different river that featured in them, a different horror.

'It got worse after . . . after you left,' Henri adds.

'I—'

'I'm not blaming you, Billie, I'm sure you had your reasons,

but after what had happened . . . Louise started to lose it. It was
. . . how can I put it? . . . I didn't understand her any more. One
evening she asked me to look at that wretched burn she had,
hidden under her hair. All of a sudden she grew serious. She
turned round, back to the mirror, lowered the top of her dress
and laid her fingers on the scar. I actually saw her stroke it. And
she talked to me about monsters . . . She asked me whether
monsters beget monsters, or something along those lines.'

'Monsters?'

'I don't know what she was driving at. I didn't try to understand, I was impatient. It was part of our history, part of her
mystery. I came to V several times that year. The relationship
carried on. And then one day I found the diary . . .'

'The diary?'

'Louise was so cross with me . . . I was sorry, but—'

'Hold on, Henri! I don't know what you mean!'

Billie jumped to her feet, knocking over the glass on the coffee
table.

'What diary are you talking about?'

It was two years after Billie had left V. Henri didn't know it then,
but this would be his last summer with Louise. He, too, would
be leaving.

Louise had found a job as a secretary at the doctor's surgery
in a nearby town. She arranged to take her annual leave to co-
incide with Henri's visits, but she wasn't always able to book
time off, especially when he turned up unexpectedly.

He would lounge in bed before heading into the village, where
he would buy a copy of the local newspaper and go and sit
outside the only café. He would order a coffee and stay there
leafing through the pages and listening to the old guys sitting
nearby. 'Bloody hell! Old Marcelle's kicked the bucket!' It was in
V that he had learnt to enjoy the quiet spells. When the heat
became unbearable he would leave the café, get some shopping
and go back and make lunch. Louise was sometimes able to come
home at lunchtime. He would be waiting for her.

That day she didn't come home: it was early summer, a lot of patients wanted a last-minute appointment before going off on holiday, and the influx of tourists was just beginning. There was one emergency after another. Henri made himself a coffee in the kitchen, picked up a magazine in the living room and went upstairs for a lie-down. He read for a bit, then had a shower. When he came back into the bedroom, he had gone to pick up his watch from the bedside table and had accidentally knocked over what was left of his coffee, spilling it on the pillow. He had gone in search of a clean pillowcase, and was rummaging around in the cupboard. It started as innocently as that. Searching among the piles of clothes and sheets, he got distracted. The cupboard was such a mess. Louise must have all sorts of treasures hidden away in there. And there was the smell of her. The heady scent of her, permeating every inch of cloth.

It was on the top shelf, reachable only by standing on a stool, that he had found the box. It was at the very back. He couldn't see it, but could feel it when he reached his arm out.

He had removed it from its hiding place: it was an ordinary box, but it was firmly sealed with several loops of sticky tape. He had hesitated, weighed it in his hand and given in. When he opened it, the box gave off a strong musty smell. Seeing what was inside – a dirty cloth – he had felt foolish and wondered why on earth he had been so desperate to know what was in there. Now he would have to put everything back as it was, hide his tracks. But then, under the fabric, he had discovered a school exercise book and some loose pages.

The paper was so old that it looked as if it might fall apart in his hands. Henri had put the box down at the foot of the cupboard, glancing briefly at the pages lying in the bottom of it, which looked like letters, and had taken the exercise book in his hand. Inside, the pages were black with tiny writing that was hard to decipher. It was a diary, and was dated. It began in 1943. Some lines were illegible. He had skimmed through several pages, noticing words at random, and what he read had made him shudder. He had come across the name Louise several times, baby Louise, and that of her father, Jacques. It talked about war as well, about blood and forgiveness. About a soldier. If he had had more time, he would definitely have wanted to read it cover to cover, because he had a feeling that he had stumbled across something of vital importance. But Louise had returned.

'What are you doing?' Her voice had made him jump. She was leaning against the door, her lips pressed together, as vivid as the red headband holding her hair back. She stood there glaring at him in her white dress dotted with flowers, which made her look deceptively youthful. 'My God, what have you done?' He had struggled to get his words out, made a stupid excuse. 'I was looking for something, Louise. I thought I'd made it fall down and—' As he was stammering his pathetic apologies, she had walked up to him, snatched the diary out of his hands and bent down to pick up the box. She was shaking, holding them close and yet away from her body, as if they were something loathsome. Then she had started crying. 'You read it! You read it! You read everything!' She couldn't stop repeating it over and over. 'No, Louise, no, I didn't read anything! I promise! And even if I had read it, what difference does it make? There's no need to get in such a state!' She had erupted in a blind rage. He vaguely made out, from the words she spat at him, that these papers were not hers, that she had found them, that there was nothing she could do about it. That she disapproved of what was in there. Those were the actual words she had used: she disapproved of those writings. Then she had fallen silent and given him a pleading look: 'What now, my love? What now?'

Henri sighs; his index finger plays with the puddle of spilt water on the coffee table.

'She started on about monsters again. She talked about curses and goodness knows what else. I listened to her raving on. I was stunned. Then she fell silent. She seemed exhausted. She stuffed the exercise book and the loose pages in her bag and told me she wanted me gone by the time she got back.'

'But what exactly was in the diary?'

'I don't know, Billie. Whatever it was, she didn't want it to see the light of day.'

'But where is it now?'

'I've no idea . . . I did what she asked and left. I knew what her rages were like, Billie. She was desperate for me to stay, but I was a coward. I left without so much as a backward glance. I left her alone with—'

'With her monsters.'

Billie looks at the spreading ring on the coffee table where the glass tipped over. She thinks about the way shockwaves radiate out across calm waters. The way they multiply and propagate from a tiny point of impact, the ripples spreading far and wide.

3

Sitting in the car – she has locked the doors from the inside – Billie waits for her hands to stop shaking. She has turned the air conditioning up to maximum, but it's no use. She is gasping for air. She puts a hand to her burning forehead, wonders which is the quickest route back to her hotel. And now a thunderstorm erupts above her head. The elements really do seem to be conspiring against her.

Henri has left. They said goodbye to each other, but it was an awkward goodbye, without physical contact, a goodbye in which everything unspoken – reminiscences, sadness, budding affection – hovered between them like an invisible hot wave.

He has stirred up so many memories, and now they are all a big jumble. She came to V to lay her own ghosts to rest, and now here she is having to deal with Louise's.

Somewhere there must be a hiding place containing a diary waiting to be opened. Or maybe it no longer exists. Maybe it was thrown out along with virtually the entire contents of the house when Louise left for Les Oliviers. Maybe she made a bonfire of it.

What might those pages contain to make Louise go berserk like that? After Henri left, Billie searched all the rooms in the house, but she found only empty cupboards and drawers. The various items brought back from Les Oliviers, which were already familiar to her, still lay on Louise's bed: an assortment of souvenirs, some clothes, a towelling dressing gown, a blanket and, in the middle, her only book, the prayer book.

She picks up her bag from the passenger seat and takes out the small book, running her hand over its worn leather. Henri's words had rattled her. When he mentioned the soldier, what Billie had taken to be a delusion on her mother's part suddenly took on a new dimension. Who could he be, for his image to haunt her even at Les Oliviers? Louise had forgotten whole chapters of her life, but not him.

And she disapproved of whatever was in those pages, or so she had repeatedly told Henri. She had not written it and she found it abhorrent. But she had kept the diary, taken care to conceal it, and continued to pray for the soldier.

Billie moves off, driving cautiously in the direction of her hotel. She ignores the beeping of horns behind her; let them overtake. The rain is now a steady patter on the windscreen. The image of Louise and Henri standing shoulder to shoulder under a porchway forms in her mind. Louise's sodden blouse, her pink skirt weighed down by the rain, lightning criss-crossing the sky, the crashes that follow, that make them jump, their wet skin touching. *God must be angry this evening!* Louise looking at Henri for the first time.

Through the misted window Billie spots the hotel sign twinkling beyond the sheet of rain. She parks, switches off the ignition and gazes at the faded façade, the cracked wall. Why exactly is she here? Why has she come all this way? She curses Henri, curses his ludicrous diary story, curses her own memories, still so vivid. It was all such a long time ago. She and Lila were just kids. Is there really nowhere you can bury your past? Until recently everything was almost simple. Everything was in order. All of a sudden she feels so tired. She tells herself she ought to pluck up her courage instead of sitting there ruminating in the thunderstorm. All she needs to do is dash through the downpour, pick up her key at reception, hurry upstairs to the shelter of her room, huddle under the covers, call Paul and tell him she desperately needs his arms around her. But she doesn't ask for things like that. Not ever. She doesn't need anyone, and especially not a man.

She jumps out of the car, her handbag above her head. Her

clothes drip in the hotel lobby as she asks for her key at reception. The clinking of glasses from the dining room sows a different idea in her mind. Would it look strange, her drinking alone here? Then again she is far from home, in the back of beyond, battling her demons. The alcohol will relax her. She sits down at the bar and orders a glass of dry white wine, with some olives to go with it.

'Can I have some more?' She is famished and the five miserable olives she has been given are never going to satisfy her hunger.

'Shall we swap?' asks the barman with a lovely smile, offering her a full dish and taking away her empty one.

Shall we swap?

You're on! We'll swap! It's a deal! Lila's hand bumped hers. Which of them had had the idea first?

It's a Saturday morning. There's no school.

The sound of the glass breaking on the tiled living room floor, at Suzanne's feet, makes them jump. Louise hurries off to get a sponge and a bag.

'There goes another one! I'm going to make us all drink from plastic cups soon, I'm telling you!' She pinches her lips together to stop herself laughing. Louise and Suzanne are kneeling down collecting up the shards of glass, while Uncle Henri hovers nearby.

Lila and Billie take the opportunity to disappear upstairs. 'It's time,' they whisper. The idea of a swap has fired their imagination. Up in Billie's room, they crawl under a sheet strung out between two chairs. The light filters through the cotton so that they sit in a halo of sunshine.

They have abandoned the idea of a razor. It wasn't designed for hair. It turned out badly when they tried it on the first of Billie's dolls. So badly that she had to hide it in the bottom of the dustbin, under some potato peelings.

They have sharpened the scissors with the big steel rod Henri uses for the carving knife. 'They need to be sharp,' Billie explained. 'Otherwise they won't cut properly and we'll end up tearing it out.'

Billie tries first. She grasps the first plait, places the blades against Lila's scalp, sticks out her tongue, closes her eyes and performs a sharp snip. Lila goes 'Ow!' A drop of red appears where the hair has been cut. 'Sorry!' Billie concentrates harder when it comes to the second plait; she holds the scissors slightly away from the head. *Snip.* Then it's Lila's turn with the scissors, but she has a harder, much more time-consuming job because Billie's hair stands out in all directions.

The hardest bit is over. Now they are both wondering what to do with their new hair. They come running out of their den of sheets, out of the bedroom, with their precious treasure in their hands, but slow down at the sight of Suzanne, who is standing rooted to the spot at the bottom of the stairs, looking at them with a strange expression. She clamps her hand over her yellow teeth and utters a kind of groan. She turns bright red. She is transformed before their very eyes.

Then Louise arrives and stands pressed against Suzanne's side, and Uncle Henri as well. 'Oh my God! Oh my God!' They look at the girls and repeat the words over and over again. They look as though they are praying, their necks craning skywards, as if in church.

Billie and Lila are suddenly on high alert. Billie is holding the blonde plaits, still held together by their blue hair elastics, in her right hand. The brown tresses are dangling from Lila's left hand. They sense the anger mounting and bubbling up down below, far from their lofty vantage point, and their free hands grasp hold of each other.

Then Suzanne storms up the stairs, grabs Lila's hand and shakes it until it releases the brown strands. Billie stares at her friend's bald head pressed between the breasts of her mother, who is swaying from side to side. She thinks about the doll hidden under the potato peelings in the dustbin, about her own pale head and the tufts of hair sticking out here and there like ears of wheat or little roots. Suzanne, holding Lila clutched firmly against her like a bag, quickly goes back down the stairs, moaning something that Billie is unable to make out. They are gone in a matter of seconds.

Downstairs, Louise and Uncle Henri are still there staring at her. The floor around her feet is strewn with handfuls of brown hair. Her hand has a firm hold of her new hair, the blonde plaits. They are hers. From now on they are her.

'Give me those, Bill!' Louise shouts as she heads up the stairs.

She is so pale. Her tan has literally dissolved, vanished in the snap of a finger, like Lila's hair gone in a snip of the scissors.

'No! It's mine! It's my hair!'

'Don't be so stupid, Billie! It's not yours! It will never be yours!'

Louise approaches, reaches for the plaits. She really does want to take them away from her. Billie can't let that happen! But Louise insists. 'Give them to me!' Billie clutches the scissors in her dress pocket and swings them randomly in the air. The point plunges so easily into her mother's wrist. The feel of the blade piercing the tender skin before hitting bone reminds her of that of a knife sinking into a lovely ripe peach – the fruit's flesh releasing its sweet juice around the hard stone.

The blade gives a silvery flash before embedding itself there, in Louise's skin. There has been a lunar eclipse at the end of Billie's arm, a wave of a magic wand that has made her wish come true. *You can't have it! It's mine!* At one end of the vivid curved line, the blood is a spreading sheaf of red, a bouquet of a hundred flaming roses.

Louise wears an expression of astonishment. And her skin! You might almost think her face was covered in a white powder, with earthy glints. The blood trickles in all directions, branching out before gathering in a red puddle at her feet.

Just before midday, she is woken by the throbbing in her head.

As she opens her eyes Billie remembers and cringes. How many glasses did she drink? She ate nothing apart from all the olives the barman kept passing her until she was sick of them.

'Are you feeling okay, miss? You ought to have something to eat.' She remembers him being quite insistent, even suggesting that someone accompany her to her room.

The pain is drilling into her head; she massages her temples. Her whole body is reeling. Hard to say which is worse at that moment – the migraine, which might well spoil most of her day, or the nausea.

She stands in front of the bathroom mirror and looks at her swollen features, her cardboard-like face. Her hair has tried to escape from the hairband holding it in place, forming a big bulge above her forehead. Whether comical or pathetic she cannot say. She doesn't look very different now from the way she looked as a child. She used to wear it that way all the time, her wild hair, her pride and joy back then. Before Lila started stirring things up. *Are you on? Shall we swap?*

She sees herself as a little bald girl in her pinafore dress standing in front of her mother, eyeing her with a look of defiance – *bad girl!* Breathless, they stand facing each other in the corridor, where a bare lightbulb hangs from the ceiling. Blood gushes from Louise's wrist, forming a pool at her feet.

Her thoughts are interrupted by the telephone ringing. 'We need the room back by one p.m., madam. The cleaners have to get it ready for the next guests,' announces the voice on the other end.

Standing at right angles to the bathroom mirror, she notices her swollen stomach. She runs her fingers over the bulge. That awful sick acid feeling in her stomach.

She sets the shower to a moderate temperature and slowly turns it down to cold. Her breathing speeds up on contact with the icy water. She thinks of the river, of Lila, of their games. Her hands rub vigorously at her skin, hoping this will help rid her of yesterday's toxins. Little by little she gets used to the temperature. She smooths the ends of her hair, strand by strand, slowly, the way Louise used to do, and stays stood under the icy jets for a long time.

4

A few days after the *swap*, they had decided to treat themselves to a special meal. It was market day in the village.

'Two punnets of strawberries for the price of one. Come on, sir, madam, it's a bargain! They're the last of my strawberries.' Louise gave a dismissive wave of the hand to show she wasn't interested.

'Can we have that one, Uncle Henri?'

Billie is pointing to a roast chicken revolving on a spit, licked by the flames below. The delicious smell has accosted her nose and she is already salivating at the thought of tucking in to the chargrilled meat.

'Can we? Can we have that one?'

'All right then, Billie, choose whichever one you want.'

Henri strokes her head. Louise had had a go at tidying up her hair and Billie let her, even though she was furious inside. The result is a kind of crew cut, like the village boys' haircuts. Without her brown mane, her yellow eyes look enormous; they almost seem to take up her whole face.

'There you go, lad, a nice chicken for you!'

In her outsized shorts, Billie knows that she looks like a boy. She shrugs her shoulders, takes the chicken and walks away, distracted by the other stalls.

'She didn't do it on purpose, did she?' Louise had asked Henri as he was attending to her dressing.

'No, of course not.' They had not said anything else. Or at least, Billie had not heard anything else.

★   ★   ★

They amble along in front of stalls crammed with all manner of goods. The village takes on a whole new character on market days, its streets a hive of activity. Roused by the shouts of the stallholders, it seems suddenly to wake from a long slumber.

They choose a red wine. To go with the lovely tender chicken, says Uncle Henri. And their bags grow heavier.

A stall of a thousand colours catches Billie's eye. She walks over to it, strokes the shimmering silk, her finger tracing the green patterns on the pink fabric. The scarf is beautiful. It seems to have been waiting just for her.

'You like it, Billie?' her uncle asks. She shakes her head, but her fingers clasp the silk.

He kneels down in front of her, folds one end of the scarf into a kind of sausage and winds it around her head. He knots the two ends together at the nape of her neck. Her cropped hair disappears under the silk. Billie wraps her arms around her uncle's neck and, for a moment, nestles her head against his shoulder. She jiggles from foot to foot as he pays the stallholder.

Henri takes her hand and they continue on their way, Billie walking along by her uncle's side in her new headgear, beaming with pride.

That was their last day together that summer. He would soon be leaving. Billie, pressing her ear to the bathroom door, had heard them talking earlier.

'Please stay a bit longer. Don't go so soon!' Louise had said.

'I'll be back before Christmas,' Henri had promised.

'Come here, help me re-do my bandage and let's make the most of the nice weather!'

Louise was doing her best to be cheerful; she had no choice. Her voice had a new, unfamiliar tone to it.

She was sitting on the edge of the bathtub facing Uncle Henri, who was unwinding her bandage. It was stained where the scab was still fragile and the wound still oozing blood. The dressing covered the whole of her wrist. Billie had heard Henri say that she would have a scar. He had disinfected the wound by dabbing it very gently, which had made Louise wince. 'That stings!' she had said, shooting him an accusing look even though it wasn't his fault.

Louise was too busy tending to her wound and cursing it to think any further about the severed blonde plaits. She imagined they had ended up in the bin. That was where they belonged. But Billie had taken advantage of all the mayhem to squirrel them away. It hadn't taken her long to decide where to put them. There was only one place: under the three loose floor tiles in her mother's bedroom.

Billie had discovered them one day as she was slithering under the bed. She had lain still for a moment on the cold floor, listening to the sounds in the house. She had slid her hand over the hexagonal tiles, humming to herself, and, as she did so, had felt a slight discrepancy in the levels under her fingers, a flaw invisible to the naked eye. The tiles were broken clean in two here, and the crack was so fine that you had to touch it to notice it. She had lifted one of the tiles and slipped her hand into the space beneath it. It was tight but would make an ideal hiding place: you just needed carefully to lift up one of the ends then lower it down in exactly the same way so that only the terracotta colour was visible.

On the day of the swap, Billie had hastily slid under Louise's bed and located the zigzag crack. She had hidden the blonde tresses there. Her treasure. No one but she would know about the plaits of hair under Louise's bed and – the ultimate irony – Louise would go to sleep directly above them every night.

The three floor tiles! How could Billie have forgotten about the three broken tiles? Her treasure is probably still in its hiding place. She had pushed it to the back of her mind, along with everything else to do with V or Lila. While the village was mourning one of its children, she had chosen to leave. Not to be part of the outpouring of grief. To get far enough away that these places and these people might never have existed.

Are they still there, those snatched pigtails, hidden under the tiles – dusty, still held together by their blue hair elastics? Dirty and scrunched up, crammed in side by side like miniature corpses?

She has three hours left until her flight back. She only has hand luggage, so she only needs to be at the airport an hour before take-off to go through customs and security before boarding. That leaves her with just over two hours to pop over to V, to the house with the low ceilings, to check whether the three broken floor tiles are still there, before heading to the airport, returning the hire car and making her way to her departure terminal. There is plenty of time.

Billie puts her clothes on over her still damp skin, shoves her belongings into her bag and swings the door of her hotel room shut, suddenly in a hurry to pay her bill at reception.

5

She bursts into the house, doesn't waste time opening the shutters, but instead gropes her way through the oddly-shaped rooms she knows so well. She takes the stairs four at a time, turns on the torch on her mobile phone to light up what was once Louise's bedroom, and, at the sight of it, has to choke back the tears that are all of a sudden gathering into a hard lump in her throat. She lies down on the floor, wriggles under the bed, her heart pounding. She touches the tiles with her fingertips, running them over the surface until she feels the raised crack down the middle of the three wobbly ones. She is ten years old again. She lifts the lid off the hiding place she alone knows, which has concealed her treasure all these years, and is ready to delve her fingers into the soft bundle of hair, to rediscover this piece of Lila that fills her with horror but that she needs to feel. Her fingers encounter a bare surface. There is nothing in the hollow, only a void. The hair must have disintegrated over the years, succumbed, as one might expect, to the ravages of time. *But wait. There actually is something in there. Something cold, hard and damp. A package.* She pulls at it, extracts it from its tomb, realises with a start what it is, and quickly puts the three hexagonal tiles back in place. She doesn't attempt to examine the package she is holding in her hands. Not right away. She clutches it to herself and hurries back down the staircase.

Billie has joined the queue and is watching the comings and goings of the aircraft on the tarmac below as the travellers inch their way towards the desk at the departure gate. She has been waiting twenty minutes already. She wishes she could control time, that she didn't have to be dependent on it.

She thinks of Paul, who is going to meet her at the airport when she arrives back in Paris – Paul who was so kind on the telephone just now, when she told him about her mother, about the funeral. She pats the package in her bag, her last hour in V still fresh in her mind.

'Thank you, miss.'

The flight attendant checks her boarding card and courteously hands it back to her. Madame or mademoiselle – it depends on who she is talking to. It is different each time, probably because Billie is at that intermediate stage when fine lines appearing on the skin offer a hint of what is to come. People often refer to it as the prime of life if they are trying to be kind, even though age is already starting to take its toll. The newly emerged butterfly spreads its wings only for a day. When evening comes it folds them again in a final tremor of happiness.

The aircraft takes off, flies out over the sea before banking around and setting a course for its final destination. Billie scans the ground for the houses of V. Her gaze alights on one of the villages they are flying over, one of the many. Seen from up here, it looks innocuous, devoid of interest.

It was there, she thinks. It was there that it all began. Everything started and still lingers in the dusty house in V, the scene of her earliest years and all that they entailed. Eating, urinating, dribbling, forming syllables, calling, whining. Howling.

She can recall her early life with remarkable clarity.

A single syllable. 'Mum.' A plastic teething toy clamped between her bare gums.

'Mum-my!'

'Don't call me that, Bill!'

A drawing gone wrong. A coloured chimney at a violent tilt. The stick of pastel that crumbled on the page, leaving bits everywhere. The sheet of paper torn up by sausage fingers.

The loneliness before Lila.

Then the games they played and the novel feeling of meaning something to someone. Of being one half of their duo. You up for it, Lila? You up for it, Billie? Cross my heart and hope to die . . .

It could have been that: just children's games.

They could have freed themselves from the march of time. Stayed put in the world of yesteryear – that perfect world – and continued on their way side by side, naive, trusting, forever united against wind and tide, two sisters pitted against the whole wide world, the pair of them inseparable. For in that world, everything was genuinely forgiven.

Hey! Billie! Lila's high-pitched voice still resonates in her head, pesters her, keeps going over the same old things. She has kept quiet for too long. *D'you want to know what Jean did to* me, *Billie? D'you want to know?* How can she banish that voice, those deadly echoes from her mind?

Once the plane reaches cruising altitude, she unfastens her seatbelt and retrieves her bag. The package resting on her knees gives off a foul smell, the smell of a vault where corpses lie. How long has it been there, hidden under the tiles? Who put it there and when? No one knew about the secret cavity except her – during her childhood years at least. She is absolutely certain of that.

The package consists of a compact object bound up in a piece of cloth that is tied in a tight knot. To start with Billie tries to unpick the knot, but she ends up tearing the fabric – it's so old it doesn't take much effort – and carefully reaches inside.

Inside the cloth is what appears to be a school exercise book. Billie runs her hand over the worn cover with its faded design. Her fingers start to tremble. Part of her already knows that what she is about to discover will change everything.

A newer sheet of paper has been tucked in under the cover, with a few words scribbled on it in a round, clumsy hand. 'This is where I come from.' Billie recognises Louise's handwriting. It's not hard: there is a bubble hovering above the 'i's.

She also notices a few hairs trapped in the centrefold of the exercise book. Wheat-blonde. Suddenly Billie is shaking all over. Her neighbour looks round at her. 'Are you all right?'

She doesn't dare touch them, but instead quickly turns over the first page of the notebook. The pages are so fragile that a breath of wind might reduce them to dust. Billie finds herself confronted with pages black with dense, jerky writing, a spidery scrawl. In some places the ink has run and the words are misshapen. Most of the pages have a date at the top. As she delves into the diary, Henri's words come flooding back to her, giving her a sick feeling. *It talked about war, about blood and forgiveness. About a soldier.*

She realises she may be about to encounter Louise's monsters.

A handful of pages have been tucked into the middle of the exercise book. Letters written on paper that seems even older, and is creased and torn in places. Billie doesn't linger over the letters. Not yet. She would rather go back to the beginning of the notebook. With her heart in her mouth, she deciphers the first page.

PART FOUR

Adele

I

8 December 1943
My God, this waiting . . . It just goes on and on.

I wait and I write letters to my young soldier that I cannot send because I have no address.

Is he alive or killed in combat, my young fighter of the Free French Forces?

When he returns, I shall give him all these letters as proof that he was in my thoughts.

I write my letters by candlelight, after I have finished my sewing jobs, with my old father snoring next to me by the stove. It is so cold.

I write for hours, and this never-ending absence makes my heart ache. When I have run out of words, when I am so exhausted that my hand shakes, I carefully fold the letter, slide it into an envelope, seal it, and go upstairs to hide the precious note under my mattress.

I slip in between the sheets that are cold with loneliness.

10 December 1943
'My love, when all this is over I'm going to take you away somewhere.' That's what the young soldier said as he set off for war, fervent and brave, gifting his love to his country rather than his sweetheart. 'We'll have a place of our own, just you wait. I'll make a wooden cradle for our baby, and I'll paint it yellow, the colour of the sun. For you, I'll bring back a rose and a dress that you'll wear for the night of our wedding.'

Those words full of hope were all he left me as he disappeared out of sight. I can still see that wave of his hand – I replay it over and over in my mind's eye. His parting gesture was a farewell tinged with pride.

I waited by the side of the road, my hand still raised. I thought he was going to come back, that he was bound to come back because the war made no sense, because Corsica had just been liberated; I thought that it would soon be our turn and that perhaps they no longer needed him. Because they were going to tell him, to confirm what was obvious – that he would be better off going back home to his sweetheart. Because that is what matters above all else. Because everything else changes. Because war is a mistake, a temporary state of affairs that steals lives and sends men insane.

I stood by the last bend and kept my eyes riveted on the dirt track until darkness fell. Once in a while I fancied I saw his silhouette coming towards me, a rose in his hand and a smile on his lips.

'My love, when all this is over I'm going to take you away some-where . . .' you told me. I stroked the woven badge sewn onto your uniform sleeve, the red Cross of Lorraine on a blue diamond, and I felt like weeping.

I am ready, I am here, we can leave right away, I don't need anything other than you. Show me the house that you spoke of, be quick and make the cradle for our child, for it is here, I can feel it inside me, I can feel the fruit of your seed growing inside me like a poppy. Or a rose. This softness in me, this fragility, a girl, it will be a girl. Come back to us, hold out your hand and give your sweetheart the rose you picked on your way back home.

So Billie has found the soldier. The one Louise used to pray for. She wants to understand, straight away. She quickly flicks through the notebook. It's virtually full: page upon page of dense writing that is hard to decipher. And yet the diarist has gone to some trouble over it. The pages are dated, with margins, the lines of writing more or less straight. But the writing becomes more and more tightly packed as it goes on. The crossed-out words are almost illegible in places. There is a kind of breathlessness to them that grows increasingly acute. An urgency.

She turns back to the centre of the notebook, where the letters are, and takes the first one in her hand. As on all the others, the ink is very nearly erased. The letters look as if they have been scrunched up – ready to be discarded, probably – but that the writer then changed their mind and tried to salvage what they could. The creases still bear hints of agitated hands, of fingers grasping the paper yet hesitating to rip it to shreds and destroy these traces that, one day, will no longer serve any purpose. Fingers that crush and then regret, that want to reinstate the words they tried to obliterate. Palms that iron out the sheets, but end up spreading the grease and dirt around. They start from scratch again, reconnect with the value of the words. For these words are a declaration. A letter should never be torn up. A letter is a form of exposure, an attempt to overcome one's shame, something that must not be destroyed.

22 December 1943

My love,

Every day I come and wait for you in the same place – the last place I saw you, that place beyond the end of the village where the road forks, disappears behind the ancient tumbledown cottage and sets out on its tortuous route across this landscape of a thousand hills.

Every day I picture again the last kiss you blew me. It feels as if only a few minutes have passed since you sent me that sign, and I keep expecting you to reappear, to lead me to our old cottage and tell me that you're not going to leave, that we will stay in this ramshackle place until the end of time.

The words you said under the rickety beams of that abandoned house, the promises you made in the place we briefly made our own . . . I think of them every day. Rather than writing them down, I try to learn them by heart and say them out loud. But my memory plays tricks on me and sometimes I can't seem to get them in the right order any more. They are there, all jumbled up, and I can no longer remember the manner in which they were said, the general drift of them. I am also worried that I may have forgotten some of them for good.

I'm sorry, but then I start being plagued by doubts. I am no longer sure that those words were really spoken, that our encounter in that derelict hut really happened. Then I touch my belly, and I feel it hard and swollen. I am carrying a part of you in me. The thought cheers me up.

Will you be here for the birth of our baby? Will you have

*returned a hero, safe and sound, by then? Will we choose a
Christian name together for our child? Did I already mention
that I have a feeling it will be a girl? That's what my body is
telling me. There is no doubt about it.*

   All my love,
   Adele

So Billie has Adele's diary in her hands. Pious Adele is pregnant
with her first child, her only child, Louise.

She is awaiting the return of Jacques, a young soldier of the
Free French Forces.

Adele, Jacques and Louise . . . She holds their story in her
hands. She strokes the worn pages, trying to focus her mind. It
takes a moment. She needs to think hard before continuing. The
pages' many creases and stains are the marks of time. Signposts
in the journey she is about to embark on.

Suddenly she is slammed violently backwards. A jolt shakes
the cabin, followed by several more. The warning lights come on
above the seats, and everywhere she can hear the metallic click
of seatbelts being fastened. Billie sees the flight attendant running
down the central aisle. Her neighbour's hands grip the armrests.
She registers the gasps and exclamations of the other passengers,
but her mind is elsewhere. The diary is still lying in her lap, and
she places her hands on top of it. Outside, the pure blue sky
looks so calm. Billie gazes into its vast expanse and tries to draw
something from it, to steady her thoughts, her stomach, the blood
pulsing through her veins. The commotion all around her is
nothing compared to the storm raging in her own body. She runs
her hand over the diary again and takes a deep breath before
plunging back in.

2 January 1944

We have had our first snow of the season.

My poor father is bed-ridden now; he coughs a lot. He has been like this for weeks. I now have twice as much to do. I look after the house and sew long into the night, but I'm getting behind with my work. I have lost a number of customers from the town – the richest ones, the most exacting ones, the ones who enabled us to earn enough money to get by each month, even during the lean war years. My fingers are stiff with the cold; I have chilblains on my hands. It helps if I sit near the stove to work.

Besides the cold we also have the rationing. There is so little available off the shelf. Butter, milk and meat are a rare treat – everything is in short supply since we have been under occupation. The Germans take everything for themselves. We survive on carrot-top soup and radish soup and I can see my father losing strength from day to day. This morning I got to the bakery too late and it had run out of bread.

Haberdashery supplies are also hard to come by. I am finding it hard to fulfil the assignments I still have in my order book. I have had to resort to bartering for my fabrics and threads – I managed to get hold of some in exchange for our 250 gram sugar ration.

My father says nothing when I arrange the pillows under his head so that he can sit up without tiring, and give him his evening meal. He drinks every last drop of the thin soup and makes no comment because he knows. He is just sorry to have become a burden.

I went to church and prayed for him. Someone told me the grocer's wife has died. She caught a cold and it turned into bronchial pneumonia. The doctor did all he could but she was too weak to fight it off. This winter is terrible. Thank goodness we have the stove . . . But how long will our supply of wood last if the cold carries on? I have already been through the house in search of anything that could serve as fuel: paper, old boxes. I even sawed up a cabinet.

If God could only hear me . . . Father has coughed up blood again. We both know what that means, but we don't talk about it. Life must go on.

I wash him and apply ointment to the bedsores all over his back. His ruined body has become alien to him. Only in his eyes, still crystal clear, does his soul still pulse. In them I can still read his strength, his peasant's hardiness. So I focus on those bright eyes. 'You're a good girl', he tells me, and wishes me a good night's sleep.

15 February 1944

My poor father is delirious. When he woke up this morning he was calling for Pierre and Lucien. My God, it's nearly four years since they left us. I had to remind him that both my young brothers died a hero's death.

There have not been many deaths among those who enlisted from V. The majority are being held prisoner in Germany. If that had been the case for Pierre and Lucien, at least we could have kept our hopes up . . .

I spend most of my time cooped up in the house. I only venture outside to go shopping and go to church. Would I be braver if Pierre and Lucien were here? Their bedroom door has remained closed since they left. I daren't open it.

Why has God called them to Him? I prayed so hard for their souls. Maybe not hard enough.

25 February 1944
Last night the snoring stopped. The sudden absence of the rattling that has accompanied me through the night for the last few weeks caused me to wake with a start. I knew what this silence meant, but I couldn't summon up the courage to get up and close his eyes. I remained lying in the dark with my gaze fixed on an imaginary spot on the ceiling, waiting for something to happen to rouse me from my lethargy. This stupor was only superficial though: beneath the surface, my heart was beating so hard I felt as though I was suffocating.

I waited until I had calmed down, clambered awkwardly out of bed, wound the strips of cloth tightly around my belly and went out at first light to fetch the parish priest. We walked back together through the deserted streets to prepare the wake.

27 February 1944
All the old people of the village attended the funeral, for my father was a respected man, a village elder, a pillar of the community. Not many young people showed up. Since conscription into the Compulsory Work Service has started, many of them have fled and are lying low on farms, in the mountains . . . wherever they can, poor things!

The tears were sincere, the sadness of this day so palpable. The old folk poured out their sorrow, hugged me in their arms and smothered me with their grief. I put on a brave face until they had all left the house.

Once I was alone, I started tidying away his belongings. I carefully folded his few items of clothing, stripped the sheets from his bed, put away the Bible that lay next to his pillow, cleared away the bits and pieces he kept in his bedside table. I stowed all the items in a large trunk and placed a sachet of lavender inside so that the scent would permeate this tomb full of memories.

By then my belly had begun to ache and I unwound the strips of cloth. I looked in the mirror at the bulge, the bump that is distorting my body. The rounder my belly grows, the heavier I am on my feet. The urgency of my situation fills me with terror. If I had known him longer, if he had married me, I could have called on others for help, I could have been looked after. But no one in the village knows. When I get too big, I will have no choice but to tell them the truth. I will have to endure their judgements alone. I know them; they will be harsh on me. At least my poor old father won't have had to suffer the shame of my predicament.

I pray for him. May his soul rest in peace.

2

Billie is weightless, anaesthetised by the warmth, lost in thought, while Paul stands nearby, having a shave ahead of the dinner to which he has been invited. She has been wallowing in the bathtub for so long that the skin on her fingers is all crinkly and the fingers themselves partially numbed. She can't bear the slightest contact afterwards. Shivers run along her arms and up her neck. When she has been soaking in water for a long time, even the softest fabric feels rough to her.

'I don't know how you can stay in there so long! It's like an oven!' Paul exclaims.

'Why don't you come and join me instead of having a go at me? You'll see how nice it is in here . . .'

He bends down towards her, leans on the edge of the bath and blows on her neck. A little cloud of foam detaches itself and floats away.

'How did it go down south, Billie? The funeral . . .'

'I told you. It was fine. A funeral like any other.'

'Why didn't you tell me about it the day it happened? You left just like that without saying a word! If I'd known about your mother, I could have . . .'

'What? Come down south with me?'

She draws her head down under the water. Submerged beneath the mound of foam, she closes her eyes, allowing her to concentrate on the one thought that is preoccupying her. When did Louise discover the diary? After the accident probably. The car crash that claimed the lives of her grandparents. *You were very little*, Henri had said. She had been barely two years old. Nothing about them had registered in her young memory.

Only their Christian names had stuck in her mind. Adele and Jacques.

Louise was young; she must have had so much to deal with . . . Sorting through their belongings, throwing away anything that wasn't worth keeping, clearing the house in V of some of its contents despite the urge to keep everything. Maybe she had found Adele's diary and letters hidden at the bottom of a cupboard, tucked inside a pillowcase or under a pile of sheets. Billie imagines how it had happened: Louise stumbled across the diary and the letters penned in dense writing. She was not planning to linger over them, but as she flicked through the pages, she realised that these were the confessions of her own mother. Adele had committed to paper the secrets she was probably desperate to share. Louise had read about the encounter, the soldier, their whirlwind romance, the shame. She had discovered a whole new side to her parents' life.

Louise had wanted to keep the diary, but didn't want anyone to find it, even though it was unlikely a burglar would be interested in a nondescript pile of pages riddled with damp. The gossip, the pettiness, the smirks of all those people pointing at you, she knew all about that. She had had Billie when she was young and alone. She knew what people were saying behind her back, what the people in V took her for: a loose woman. Similarly, what worried her was not so much the content of the diary but what her neighbours would make of it if they found it.

And then one day she had happened to discover the crack running across three of the hexagonal floor tiles, just as little Billie had done years previously. Had she noticed the broken tiles while she was doing the cleaning – her cloth might have snagged on it – or as she was picking up something from under the bed? However it happened, as she lifted the tiles she must have been astounded to uncover two blonde plaits covered in dust and crud. Billie can hardly bring herself to imagine the cruelty of that moment when Louise realised what it was that she had found. What must she have felt at the sight of those last relics of Lila? How long was it before she took the decision to throw them away? Had she eventually overcome her revulsion, picked up the faded blonde plaits and disposed of them?

Then, as Louise was mulling everything over, it had occurred to her that this hollow would make an ideal hiding place for the diary. A perfect tomb to house Adele's memories.

There were a few hairs left behind. And Louise had written the words: *This is where I come from.*

'I need to get going . . .'

Yes, she needs Paul to get going. As soon as he has closed the door behind him she will haul herself out of the bath, not even taking the time to dry herself before she goes to fetch the diary. She can't wait to immerse herself in Adele's and Jacques's story again, to take up where she left off.

In the meantime Billie watches Paul standing next to her, shaving, at the washbasin, where there are a few hairs floating in the water. She observes the sweep of the razor, the way his arm moves. He rubs his hand over the mirror in a circle to wipe away the condensation. But it is not long before a new film of steam clouds his reflection.

He tells her again that she is mad to be taking a bath in this heat.

But she needs to do this: to submerge everything, shroud it in mist. To obliterate her deeds, the things she has done, so that she can return to her comfort zone where she is safe.

If only it were that simple.

27 May 1944
My love,
*Where are you? What are you doing? Your absence is weighing on
me more and more. Never before have I felt such loneliness. I am
alone, my father has gone, you have gone.*

*The waves of arrests are continuing, the summary executions,
whole families have been packed off . . . There is fighting in the
scrubland – I sometimes hear the sound of machine gun fire in the
hills. Recently there have been aircraft flying overhead, at night
especially. Apparently there have been bombings and instances of
sabotage throughout the region. Refugees are pouring in from all
sides, like in 1940 when France was still split in two. V seems to
have been spared, but how long will this miracle last? First it was
Marseille and Toulon, then Cannes . . . They say something is
brewing. Now that Corsica has been liberated, will it be our turn
next?*

*I cannot bring myself to believe that you have been killed in
one of those ghastly quagmires.*

I feel your energy, I feel that you are alive.

*Will this war ever be over? Will you come back to me,
afterwards, once this madness has ended? Will everything revert
to how it used to be?*

*Will you come and see our daughter? I can feel her kicks
during the night. You would like that, to place your hand on me
and feel the life inside me. You could touch her little feet, her
head through my skin.*

*My belly has grown round, so I bind wide strips of fabric
around my waist, under my blouses.*

Come back, my love, come and save my honour before they discover my condition. I don't know how much longer I can carry on with these bindings crushing my abdomen. I am in pain. I am bent over when I sew, which increases the pressure on my belly. I bled once, just a little, but I was so afraid.

Are you on your way back?

Tomorrow I will tell them. I will go out without my swaddling. I will let them see my condition. I don't care what they might think. Our night was a night of love. They can't deny that.

I have no choice. I'll soon be seven months gone, and she is moving more and more. I cannot give birth to her alone. I need the doctor, I need the neighbours to hear when I call.

I shall hold my head up high. And I shall tell them that I am awaiting your return, that we are going to get married, that we are going to live in a pretty house on the outskirts of the village, with our child. Maybe they won't be too hard on me.

I have been with you every day and every night since you left. I am with you as you march, and in the fields drenched in the blood of war.

All my love,
Adele

29 July 1944

Louise was born in the early hours of 22 July, her crumpled face lit up by the first glimmers of dawn. I knew from the violent kicking in my belly that she would come on time. I wasn't mistaken. My baby was strong, in a hurry to come into the world. I went into labour in the middle of the night. The pain was excruciating but it didn't go on for long. The doctor said it was an easy birth. When he placed her in my arms, the sun was rising and I told myself it was a new day full of hope. I felt her tiny heart beating beneath my fingers and I wept. I knew that, from that day on, I could bear anything, with courage, for the sake of this tiny being whom I feed, wash and keep warm.

The doctor said he would come back a few hours later to check that everything was all right with the baby and me. I told him there was no need, that everything would be fine. 'I will take good care of my baby,' I said. 'She is healthy, she does not need you to come back. Just look at her cheeks and her chubby arms. We want to be alone now. I want to talk to her for hours and hours, to feed her, give her the precious milk my body has produced for her.'

In the days that followed, we fell into a pattern. Whenever she started to grizzle, I got up and fed her despite my exhaustion, despite the sleepless nights that left me shattered.

Louise suckles greedily with her little mouth, eager to strengthen her barely formed newborn body. The milk just keeps coming. Day by day I see my baby growing, blossoming like a flower.

She has fat cheeks. She has chuckles and beaming smiles for me. The rest of the world no longer exists: I give no thought to the judgements of the villagers, our meagre, dwindling savings, the sewing jobs waiting for me, or the absence of my missing soldier.

I traded some fabric for a bit of butter and some eggs. I have lost a lot of weight since the start of the war, especially since we have been under occupation. But now Louise is here. She needs to be properly fed.

The war will soon be over, my Louise, you will not grow up under the shadow of war. You will not know the smell of blood and death, you will not know the absence of a loved one who has gone off to fight. We will have something to live on — I will work hard to make sure of that. I will teach you to read, and to sew. The two of us will be happy in this house. We will share everything, always.

30 July 1944
My love,
Our little Louise is here.

She is so strong.

When the doctor placed her on my chest, the pain disappeared.

Childbirth is something so pure.

My body is empty now. I can feel the void.

But I see her, so pretty in her cradle.

Her skin is the same colour as my milk.

She is a china doll. Sometimes I am afraid she might break in my arms.

She is quiet at night.

She seems so contented, especially when I wash her.

That is her favourite time. She likes the feel of the warm water.

Her little body floats in the bath on one of my hands. I use my other hand to trickle water over her head. I stroke her forehead with my wet fingers.

She looks at me intently.

She is quiet.

There is only the sound of our breathing.

It is heart-rending to have to lift her out of the tub.

She cries and nothing will soothe her.

Neither my arms nor my milk.

Love,
Adele

3

Ten days have passed since the funeral. Ten days in which she has made no progress. Billie has a meeting coming up at Rue des Rosiers to go over the exhibition plans: the final concept, the name of the exhibition, the number of works, their dimensions, the layout, the design of the title cards . . . The date of the private view and the countdown schedule will be finalised. The press officer will be able to start promoting the event.

She has told them about the last canvas that is still in progress, the one that is the final piece of the jigsaw, the piece that will make it all make sense. The truth is that she has nothing and there is nothing in the pipeline. Those monochrome canvases covered in charcoal-drawn faces that have been piled up against the living room wall for months suddenly appear to her in a new light. She can no longer see the point of them.

She thinks about the birth of Louise. About that china doll who lights up those dark days. It occurs to Billie that she could respond to this birth in her own way. That she could add Louise to the thinkers portrayed in her artworks.

She paces around the flat, sends Paul a message, avoids looking at the sketchbook lying open on her work table, her blank page. She calls the estate agent to find out the latest on the sale of the house in V. He tells her what she already knows. There haven't been any viewings yet, but he is not at all worried. They will come, because it is in a very popular area, the house has a certain old world charm, is in good condition overall, and the price is right. The place will need updating, of course, but no major works. And, for the more adventurous, it offers plenty of scope to reconfigure the layout. Walls could be taken down to create a nice space. He talks about light wells and Billie feels a physical pain at the thought of anyone messing around with her house. She thanks him, hangs up, pours herself a glass of white wine, and waits for the alcohol to relax her before sitting down at her work table.

She raises her head and leans back to gauge the empty space on the page. She deliberates over the proportions, identifies the centre of gravity. Then she launches into it. A flush of excitement surges up from deep inside her, brings colour to her cheeks, as it does whenever she is embarking on a brand new work. Her wrist springs into action.

The first charcoal line appears. The proximal, middle and distal phalanges. The index finger is there, curled in, followed by the middle finger. The hand is taking shape, slightly puffy around the palm.

Flexing. Straightening. The structures start to form beneath the skin. The joints begin to move. The hand is alive.

The wrist is suggested by the play of shadow and emerges from the page as if from rough grass. A white line, irregular and swollen, runs across it. This line is crucial. Without it, this is not Louise's hand: it is just a hand like any other.

Billie makes the scar even more prominent by shading around its edges. She blows away the loose dust, but the white line appears and disappears, struggles to find the right shape. Yet Billie knows that mark so well. After all, it was she who made it.

Bad girl!

She tries to highlight it by going over the same place with the eraser several times, but the charcoal smears, the line grows indistinct and Louise's hand becomes an ordinary hand. Billie goes over its outlines again.

Go away! Bad girl!

The charcoal snaps between her fingers. She tears out the page with a sharp jerk, crumples it into a ball and hurls it at the window as hard as she can.

15 August 1944

*There is fighting in the area. The sound of gunfire is creeping closer
and the sky is red from the fires breaking out all over the place. We
keep ourselves closeted away, Louise and I.*

*In the midst of all this chaos, I have received a new order: for a
wedding dress! So there is still love in times of war! The dress will
be made from a gorgeous fabric I bought long ago, and will come
with a light gauze veil. My fingers trembled as I touched it. For a
moment I forgot the sounds of explosions ringing out from the hills,
the denunciations, the disappearances.*

*I thought about my soldier while working on this dress and told
myself that war does not take everything from us, that hope is still
possible.*

29th August 1944

This morning I was woken by noises and shouts from outside. I didn't dare open the window. I lay still for a long time waiting for something to happen. When I listened harder, I heard the singing and I realised we had been liberated.

I went out into the street with Louise, and I heard what it was that people were shouting: Hyères, Ramatuelle, Sainte-Maxime, Saint-Raphaël! The allies have landed! Fréjus, Draguignan, Aix-en-Provence, Toulon, Marseille! They've liberated Provence!

Jubilation in the village streets. Skinny figures dancing and singing. Has the world stopped whispering, then?

I hugged little Louise to me. I kissed her porcelain skin that looked so very white under the blazing sun. Will he come back? Will he come back?

20 September 1944

The Provence landings have not delivered us from all our woes. We are hungry. There has been no end to the shortages, and fighting is continuing in the region. They say there are still numerous pockets of German resistance. Now that the rejoicing has settled down, the newspapers are filled with talk of a purge.

My soldier has not returned. Has he perished somewhere on the coast? Is he still fighting with the maquisards?

We are living in a world in ruins and the bereaved are everywhere.

I have heard reports of women whose heads have been shaved after they were accused of sleeping with Germans. While we were singing of freedom, all over the place these traitors were being hauled out of their houses, dragged along the street and their heads shaved in the public square. I was told about one who knelt down, clutching her little boy's hand, while the people she had grown up with spat on her.

Evil is everywhere. It seems to have seeped into the earth itself.

4

'You never talked to me about her.'
    'What? About who?'
'About your mother . . .'
Paul's arms tighten around Billie.
'You never asked me about her either.'
She wriggles free of him, leans over the bed and picks up her t-shirt.
'I'm thirsty. Do you want a drink?'
'Hey! Come here!'
He grabs her by the wrist and tugs her down onto the bed.
'This time there's no escaping!'
'What d'you want me to say? There's nothing to tell. I hadn't seen her for years. The last time, she didn't even recognise me. She'd lost her marbles.'
'I'm sorry, Billie. I didn't realise.'
Paul slackens his grip.
'It's fine. That's how we always were, distant from one another, even when I was little. So you see, basically nothing has changed. And she's probably better off where she is now.'
'Billie the tough nut. Billie the loner.'
He sighs, trails his finger down the bridge of her nose.
'You don't need anyone, right . . . ?'
She shudders, escapes from his arms.
'If I'd had to rely on anyone else, I would've lost my marbles long ago too.'
She is pulling on her t-shirt and her words are muffled by the fabric.
'Sorry? What did you say, baby?'

He raises his voice, but she has already gone out of the bedroom. There is the sound of glasses clinking in the kitchen, the refrigerator door opening and closing.

Paul has left, and once again it feels to Billie as if he wasn't really here – that for him, this night spent at her flat in Rue du Repos was merely a temporary stopover. Paul has gone back to his life and Billie is definitely not part of it. It was the same with Henri, when he used to visit them in the summer. As a teenager she had been so quick to pass judgement on Louise. How naïve she had been.

Her telephone vibrates and she reads the brief message from Paul. She doesn't reply. Not yet. Instead, she strips the sheets from the bed, stuffs them in the drum of the washing machine and selects a rapid wash cycle. She collects up the plates and glasses and throws away the leftovers of yesterday's dinner. Suddenly everything seems dirty and untidy to her. The mess in her flat reminds her of the grimy state of her old home in V, the stale air in the cramped house. Billie cannot work, cannot think straight in the midst of this chaos. She throws the windows wide open, lets in the scorching summer air. Never mind the heat; she needs to air the place, get it clean. Her body is not the only thing straining under the pressure of forces from within. The flat too, the streets, the cemetery, Paris. Everything is swollen.

28 November 1944

The bedroom door is ajar and I can hear my baby's regular breathing as I alter a blouse. Louise is four months old already. She is asleep. I find it reassuring to hear her breathing. It helps me stay strong, helps distract me from the biting cold.

All night long the icy wind has been whistling furiously down the alley, stealing through gaps in the window frames, gradually chilling the entire house. I bundled Louise up in a big shawl and pulled a wool bonnet over her ears. I lit a fire to supplement the heat of the stove. I sawed up a table and placed the smallest pieces in the fireplace first. It's so bitterly cold in the house that they took an age to catch light.

I have been sewing since dawn. My fingers are chapped from the cold, and handling the needle and threads makes it worse. This is promising to be another terrible winter.

But we have been visited by an angel. Just now, shortly before midday, there came the sound of knocking at the door. I jumped to my feet and glanced into the bedroom, where Louise was sleeping with curled-up fists. I hesitated before opening the door, because in these unsettled times it's not good to be a woman on your own, isolated from the rest of the world as I am. But when the knocks came again, I was reassured by their timidity.

The man standing in front of me was tall and sturdily built, but I noticed that he was wringing his hands. 'Morning, Miss Adele. Brought you this. It's cold and I reckoned, what with the littl'un, you'd be needing to heat the place better.' The carpenter's son, someone I have been vaguely aware of for as long as I can remember. We don't know each other, even though we both grew up in the village. He was standing there in front of me, that familiar stranger, with a wheelbarrow full of logs. An unexpected gift. Standing on the doorstep of my house in the depths of this icy winter, I felt like weeping with joy and clasping his hands in mine. He kept his head down though. 'Babies don't like the cold, you know, Miss Adele.'

So I opened my door wide, I accepted his offering and my loneliness was dispelled on the spot by this gift. He arranged the logs next to the fireplace to make it easy for me to lift them across to the grate. It means I now have a decent supply of wood, so our home will be nice and cosy for the next few days. 'Well I'll be on my way now, Miss Adele.' He rubbed his blackened hands on the rough fabric of his trousers. I thanked him repeatedly, and the sight of me smiling at him like that seemed to startle him.

Before he left, I asked him if he would like to come and look at my sleeping daughter. He could peep into her cradle and see her lost in her dreams, but he would have to be as quiet as a mouse as it would be a shame to wake her. All at once the slight coarseness of his manner was gone and he approached softly. I smiled at the sight of this giant taking such dainty steps. And when he saw the two little curled fists, the blonde hair fine and soft as down framing her round cheeks, her porcelain skin, her blue eyelids, he couldn't help but give a smile of delight. He was struck by Louise's beauty, but that is no surprise, for surely no one could remain unmoved by the sight of her. There is no child in the world more beautiful.

8 December 1944

The angel knocked on our door once again. He brought more supplies of wood and handed me a bundle of items wrapped in cloth before he left.

'Can't stop, Miss Adele. My father's got work waiting for me.'

When I untied the knot holding the cloth together, I was astounded to discover a pot of jam, three eggs and some rye bread. An angel is watching over us, my Louise. Look what he has brought us. From now on we will no longer be alone. He will be back, you'll see, he will grow accustomed to us and we will bring him out of his shell.

3 January 1945

You see, my Louise, remember what I told you? He came back, and he is starting to stay for longer when he visits. Yesterday he finally agreed to sit down by the fire with me and we had a drink of warm milk together.

It is doing me good, I cannot deny it, for apart from the visits of our guardian angel, we stay cooped up in our house, cut off from the rest of the world.

8 April 1945

My love, I was walking with our daughter along the dirt track at
the end of the village ~~when you~~

    I wrapped her in a big shawl and tied the ends around my shoul-
ders and my back. She slept nestled against my chest. I walked and
she was rocked by the gentle rhythm of my footsteps. Maybe she was
dreaming that a wave had scooped her up from the ground and was
buoying her towards the soft sand, that she was floating.

    I saw your silhouette coming towards me. I have seen this scene so
many times before. It has haunted me for months. Could this be another
of those mirages? The spring sunshine dazzled me and made your
outline look blurred. The sun's rays were beating down on my eyes
and eating into your body. I could hardly make out that ~~emacia~~ *thin*
shadow approaching ever so slowly. The limping gait, the stiff body,
the head so large compared to the skinny body supporting it. Was it
you, looking so real, that stranger holding out his bony hand to me?
Will the smell of war that still clings to you follow us into our bed,
haunt our nights?

    You came closer, there was no doubt you were real, but the harsh
light of these early spring days prevented me from seeing your face.
At first I could not make out your ~~horr~~ *ravaged features. Later you*
told me about the shell, the whistling sound of the incoming shell, the
flying shrapnel, your friends falling to the ground close by, their bodies
bleeding, their limbs ~~brok~~ *scattered all around you. You were drowning*
in their blood. The pain in your leg, the blood on your face: an animal
scream erupted from you.

    The emptiness, later, when you woke up in a hospital bed, when
you felt the warm breath of the nurse bending over you changing the

bandages on your festering wounds. The emptiness in your face, the sewn-up skin which you touched with the tips of your trembling fingers.

I admit, my love, I admit that I closed my eyes when the sun's glare was gone, when I first beheld you, your head tilted down towards me. The sight of your shattered face was too much for me. The skin ~~patched up~~ *after a fashion, gaps here and there like a* ~~spoi~~ *jigsaw puzzle. And in the midst of this heap of ruins, your shipwrecked gaze seeking me out as I stood there shaking.*

Louise woke up; she had caught the smell of her father. You wished you could hide your face and instinctively placed your hand in front of your mouth. You were afraid of frightening her, you were afraid that your daughter would recoil in the same way as everyone else you passed, that she would have the same ~~very sligh~~ *instinctive reaction others have had at the sight of you.*

But Louise smiled at you. And then you cried, you let your sorrow pour out of you like a never-ending fountain.

Adele, Jacques, the war.

His injuries. The disfigured soldier.

Jacques's grotesque face . . . Billie racks her brain. Her heart is racing. She has never once heard anyone mention his face. She was too little, she has no memory of the two of them. Louise never spoke of them. All traces of them had been erased from the house in V, that is what Henri had told her.

Had Billie ever seen a photo of this heroic grandfather, this soldier of the Free French Forces disfigured in combat?

No, for as far back as she can remember, there were no pictures or mentions of the war, of injuries, of a grandfather with a shattered face. Billie had instead had in her mind the image of a sturdy man, twirling Louise around when she was little. Louise bursting with love. Never anything else, never any pain. Never any drama.

It has been dark for hours now. Billie reads, perched on one of the kitchen bar stools, her head bent over the diary, under the fluorescent light. She stretches, rubs her aching neck, walks over to the sofa and puts the diary down beneath the lamp on the coffee table. Deciphering the scrawl requires infinite patience.

She turns the page, delves back into the disjointed writing, which is becoming increasingly ragged and twitchy. Tortured handwriting, surely very different from that of the old Adele. The Adele from before the war. This Adele seems to be censoring herself. She crosses out words, battles with herself as she writes: only a lingering sense of defiance gives her the strength to carry on.

One page. Just one more page. To understand.

5

The shrill ringing goes on and on. She stands up, casts an eye around the living room until she spots her telephone. Her head is throbbing with a migraine. She spent part of the night deciphering the diary, before falling asleep on the sofa at dawn.

'Billie?'

'Yes?'

'We're waiting for you . . . We're all here!'

The planning meeting for the exhibition is this morning. How could she have forgotten?

'I'm on my way! I . . . I'm just coming!'

She quickly gathers up her things, throws on a pair of jeans, a blouse and a jacket to make herself just about presentable. She hurriedly hails a taxi on Boulevard Ménilmontant; she will never make it to Rue des Rosiers in time if she takes the metro. In the cab she ponders what she is going to tell them. How she is going to explain that she has nothing to show them, that her work has ground to a standstill, that she is incapable of carrying on with the project she had embarked on with such enthusiasm? She has grown weary of her charcoal faces, the gloomy thinkers who are supposed to be gracing the gallery's walls this winter. Something else is haunting her now: the lines of writing that she still has in her head.

'Sorry I'm late. What a morning I've had!' She ignores the glances at her crumpled clothes, her wild hair and the circles under her eyes.

'I managed to leave my portfolio behind in the taxi!'

The look of exasperation in their eyes . . . 'I had various things to show you,' she adds, 'interesting things . . . I'll email them to you . . .'

She will let them talk through the layout, discuss how to display her canvases to best effect, check that the overall concept works. After all, it is only her final piece that is missing.

Words. Persuading, justifying, debating. It always ends up as a kind of never-ending monologue. The meetings often finish without any progress having really been made.

Words overwhelm her, exhaust her. Her determination soon wavers. Billie abandons her figures to their own existence. She likes to communicate through visual images. What could be more powerful? Words can only ever be peripheral to the pictures she has dreamed up, those forms that always float within arm's reach. They hover in her mind's eye until she picks one of them and captures it on paper. She has to take her time. The image has to be born, to emerge little by little. Each touch must follow an invisible pattern to achieve a harmonious whole. Each detail is part of something bigger, as with Adele's diary. Behind the despair and the scrawled writing, a kind of implacable logic is gradually emerging. The protagonists are on hand, things are falling into place and nothing can stop what is about to happen.

'When can you show it to us, Billie?'

'Sorry?'

'I was asking whether you're on track to meet the deadline. When will we get to see the rest of your—'

'Next week! Just as I promised!'

10 September 1945

~~I have~~ *It has been such a long time since my last entry . . .*

The war is over, Hitler is dead and Germany capitulated four months ago, ~~I have~~ but a different war is now being waged within the walls of our home.

When he came back, I ~~hop~~ thought about the letters, but I didn't to give them to him. I haven't even mentioned them to him. Once he was here with me again they became pointless. Only now do I understand that I made a mistake.

I am writing this upstairs, in our bedroom overlooking the alley. I will be able to see him returning from here.

~~Where do I sta~~

Let's go back . . .

I thought that life would pick up where it had left off, that it would carry on as before. I returned to the old cottage to breathe in the blissful smells of our past. I got dust all over my clothes, my hair, I was covered in it, but it didn't feel the same as the night we spent there. And yet the mouldy beams above our heads, the mild late autumn air that seeped in through the holey floorboards – it was all so fresh in my mind. I longed to put behind me the shock of your departure, the strain on ~~me~~ my nerves from your absence. I wanted the whole period you were away to disappear, that spell of loneliness to be eclipsed by the joy of our reunion.

After our wedding, we stayed in the house where I grew up. It was easier. The house of my childhood has become that place of our own that you promised me. I thought we would have a ~~qui~~ peaceful life here, that we would be spared any more upheaval now that we were together again. I resumed my sewing with renewed determination and soon worked my way through the backlog I had accumulated after Louise's birth. You offered your services in the village and took on a few jobs working in the fields in exchange for meagre pay. We had to tighten our belts, but at the time it didn't matter. It was enough for the three of us to be together. For me at any rate.

Yes, we did have a few days' peace together. A few weeks . . . Not even a whole season.

That was before the nightmares took hold of you, before you started waking up at night drenched in sweat and shaking with ter *the cold, babbling nonsense, your eyes wide with fright. I tried to get you to talk, I tried to listen to you, to understand the evil that had wormed its way into you. But it wasn't long before you clammed up again and averted your eyes from me. In the end, you seemed to forget about the two of us who shared a home with you.*

The distance between us, the shadows under your eyes, the way you drift around the house like a sic *ghost. My love, where have you gone?*

30 October 1945
*I found the butterflies. I was rummaging through the sideboard in
the living room (in search of the brandy he hides all round the house
– our precious savings, for pity's sake!) and I found the butterflies I
used to hunt.*

It's quite a morbid sight, to be honest. So cruel.

*Louise was amazed at their ~~colour~~ shimmering wings. She is too
young to understand that they are dead, ~~crucif~~ pinned inside their
frame.*

*I used to hunt them in the woods. I wanted to be able to look at
them and compare their patterns any time I liked.*

*As I held Louise in my arms, I recalled the telling-off I had had
from my father: They're God's creatures, leave them be!*

Am I now paying the price for my ~~si~~ cruelty?

Billie, too, had once felt that urge to hunt butterflies.

She and Lila had dug out an old net. It had a hole on one side but it would do: the hole wasn't big enough for the insects to escape.

It was late afternoon when she set out. It was that mellow time of day when everything is still, the hills are bathed in an orange light and the sun no longer burns you, but instead envelops you with supreme tenderness.

In those late afternoons Billie felt strong. It was as though all of a sudden she was becoming part of the landscape, becoming one with it. Had she known how to draw back then, she would probably have depicted herself as an animal. A lioness.

She spotted a magnificent specimen perched on a lavender bush. It had large black and white stripes, and small red and blue markings on its tail end. A Scarce Swallowtail. She had learned the names of the different species of butterfly from a book at school.

Her hand gripped the handle of the net, raised it infinitely slowly. She must not let the movement disturb the stillness of the surroundings. She concentrated, inched closer, watching the way it twitched its open wings for balance.

She whipped the net down. The butterfly struggled for a moment. It went through her mind that it would damage its wings if it kept doing that.

She held the open end of the net against her front. That way she should be able to get it home without it escaping.

Billie was so proud of her catch. Never for a moment could she have imagined the reaction it would elicit from Louise.

Billie burst into the house, raced up the stairs taking them four at a time and hurtled into her mother's bedroom. Louise was lying on her bed staring at the ceiling. Billie brandished the net under her nose. 'Look! It's a Scarce Swallowtail!' She spread her little hand across the opening, as wide as it would go, to prevent the butterfly escaping.

At first Louise said nothing. She looked at Billie, then looked at the butterfly. Then looked at her again.

As her mother did not seem to understand what Billie was showing her, she repeated, more slowly: 'It's a Scarce Swallowtail.'

Louise looked like someone waking from a slumber. She sat up and took the net, or rather she snatched it from her hands, yelling 'Leave it be. It's one of God's creatures!'

She had started shaking the net wildly in all directions to get the butterfly to escape. But the insect kept colliding with the mesh. It was now impossible to tell whether it was beating its wings, or whether it was Louise's hysterical shaking that was making it dance around in the net. 'Stop it!' Billie shouted. 'You're hurting it!'

And the butterfly was finally freed. It fell to the floor. It was so light that it made not the slightest sound on landing.

It was lying on its side. One of its wings beat again, for a few seconds, then went still.

Louise and Billie, breathless both of them, could not bring themselves to look at each other. So they had kept their eyes fixed on the drama that was playing out at their feet, the butterfly's final moments.

Billie had not cried, even if she was howling inside. She never cried. She was a soldier. A lioness.

1 November 1945
~~The days are~~

The cross ~~yo~~ we have to bear. How many days has it been?

Even Louise's smiles ~~no to~~ don't warm your heart now. You now regard any sign of happiness as something obscene. Punches give you relief, brandy quenches your thirst, spite brings you contentment. It is as if this is the price you are paying for your heroism in combat.

Your breath that reeks of alcohol when you come and lie down beside me in the middle of the night, your animal grunts, the bitter, poison-filled words you spit at me. ~~Slowl~~ I am distancing myself.

I am coming to ~~des~~ hate you.

Hatred. The flip side of love. The brutal reversal that turns you into a monster . . . Billie knows it only too well. Her lips are suddenly dry. Her blood is starting to simmer as it used to during the hottest heatwaves of her childhood. She stands up, leaves the diary open on the sofa. The blood is pulsing in her temples. She pours herself a glass of white wine and opens one of the living room windows. A warm breeze wafts in.

The cemetery is a glorious sight in late afternoon on a summer's day. The sun has begun its descent; its rays filter in at a low angle between the leaves of the trees and cast pools of bronze light on the ground. *I am coming to hate you.* The words make her head pound. Billie tries to spot the statue amidst the headstones. The woman crouched over her two funeral wreaths. Twins.

They are thirteen years old. They are still friends and they are swimming.

Two sisters. Two tomboys who think they are water nymphs. The sky above V is an uninterrupted expanse of perfect blue. Under the pure cyan, the river is flat. Billie and Lila swim across it in front crawl, piercing its surface with arms taut as a bow. They arrive back from their swim with their cheeks red from the sun. 'There hasn't been a summer this hot in years!' says Suzanne, who is sitting, dressed in a roomy embroidered cotton tunic, with her elbows propped on the kitchen table, holding out a chilled lemonade for each of them with ice cubes floating in it. She watches the youngsters sipping their drinks. 'Are you staying here tonight?' Billie, with her nose in her glass, nods yes.

Later, lying on their fronts on the cool living room floor, Billie and Lila are working their way through the collection of Hitchcock films and bingeing on ice cream. Vanilla, strawberry, pistachio, chocolate, the lot. Outside, stars twinkle in a sky black as ink. They have left one of the windows open in the living room to let some air in. Billie, glued to the old television screen, feels shivers running deliciously up her arms as the shower curtain is violently swept to one side. An enormous carving knife is poised to slice into the stomach of the woman standing there naked. Before the bloodbath, the woman's striking blonde hair, wet from the shower, fills the screen. Her pallor is accentuated by a subtle hint of blusher and her bright lipstick. Then the music picks up. *Dong. Dong.* The threatening figure hovers over her, becomes a grimacing mask, the strands of her hair plaster her forehead, a scream escapes from her wide-open mouth, lipstick mixed with saliva is smeared across her cheek. Then comes the first stab of the knife, and after that the blows rain down. Shivers go up and down Billie's spine, her stomach lurches. Late into the night she is still feasting on ice cream cornets and squirming in terror at the sight of all the other hapless victims dropping dead, one after the other, having been attacked by vicious birds, madmen, perverts, maniacs of every description hidden in dark alleys, fierce creatures lurking in doorways, awaiting their prey.

Victims of bizarre punishments. Their only mistake was to have been in the wrong place at the wrong time. Their sheer bad luck held a fascination for her.

6

I ~~can't~~ don't write any more. I stride through the countryside. My solitary walks are turning into a battle, with him and with myself. These energetic hikes are my way of venting my feelings, and I return from them so exhausted and dull-headed that I can no longer think straight. For a few minutes, I am able to forget the ~~mons~~ man who shares a home with me.

I bind my daughter to my chest. I draw the shawl tight so that she is safe and snug. I leave what used to be our cosy nest, which is now a place haunted by hatred and regret. I run with Louise in my arms; we get far enough away that we can no longer hear the damned murmurs and shouts that fill the house, that impregnate the very walls and turn everything to poison.

I cut across the fields, the brambles ~~lash at~~ scratch my legs, drawing blood. The pain of the scratches on my skin distracts me from the pain in my heart and ~~hel~~ gives me some relief. I sing a summer song for Louise and stroke her chestnut locks. Her hair is darkening. It is no longer the blonde it was when she was a baby.

> *As I was walking*
> *By the clear fountain . . .*

Eventually a sense of peace ~~settl~~ comes over me, giving me fresh ~~ho~~ courage. I try to persuade myself that, if I pray hard enough, a flash of lucidity will bring my husband back to life, that for our sake he will leave the battlefields that he revisits every night and return to our embrace. But I soon sweep these hopes aside and come to my senses, for my love for that man is dead ~~and buri~~, never to return. Then the ground gives way under my feet again. And I resume my penitent's walk, feeling more desperate than ever.

3 March 1946

A hesitant, wavering ~~silh~~ shadow is crouching at the edge of the wood. I have seen that shadow before. It follows me but I am not afraid. Nowadays I am afraid only of the man who shares my bed, whom I fall asleep next to, not knowing, in light of his ~~crue~~ madness, whether I will still be in one piece when morning comes.

Surely nothing worse could befall me in this wood. I know how to defend myself. With Louise held close to me there will be two of us, and we will ~~defea~~ bring down our enemy.

I have come across him unexpectedly on several occasions on my walks. I have noticed his kindly aura. When I meet that gaze ~~ting~~ resting on me I notice that I start to warm up.

I think I come back to life at the sight of the shadow lying in wait behind the forest foliage.

~~The life shadow~~ Will it be there next time?

~~I have~~

2 April 1946

I stopped under the big pine tree, which shaded us from the sun. I untied the shawl where it was knotted behind my neck and freed Louise, who had fallen asleep. I made a soft bed for her by laying the shawl on top of the carpet of pine needles. I lay down a little way from her, in the shade of the tree, on a cushion of moss. ~~I had my~~ My head felt hot and heavy from the walk.

I didn't open my eyes when I heard him (the ~~crunch~~ twigs and pine needles crunched under his feet), nor when I felt his breath like a burning wind on my cheek. I let him unfasten the buttons of my dress, slide the cotton fabric aside, touch my skin. My heart felt ready to explode. Only then did I open my eyes. I wished this moment could last for ever. Jacques's brown hands seem to possess magical powers. Beneath his coarse shirt, such gentleness . . . A delicious ~~spa~~ breach to step into.

Tomorrow! That is all we said to one another. 'Tomorrow, Miss Adele,' he said, all awkward again. Then he stood up and left. It took me some time to regain my composure.

I was slow walking home this evening. I hugged Louise in my arms, my stomach felt tight, my breasts hard. I felt no ~~remorse~~ shame. I have betrayed no one because, for a long time now, I have had no husband. He is nothing but ~~a madman~~ a stranger living under the same roof as me, a man without a mind and without a heart.

Our angel has returned. Jacques. God has sent him back to me.

Our encounter in the shade of the forest is going to lend new meaning to my life. I am already looking forward to tomorrow.

Billie stops: she needs to pause her reading for a moment, to go back and check.

Perhaps she is mistaken. Perhaps she has misunderstood because of the wine, because of this writing that is so hard to decipher, with the muddled lines and the words crossed out.

But no, she has understood perfectly well and her heart is pounding again. She takes a few minutes to assimilate what she has just read: on the one hand there is her grandfather, a young injured soldier who has lost his mind. On the other, Jacques, the wartime angel, the encounter in the shade of the forest.

Henri, Jacques . . . How many lies? How many second-rate fathers?

When a woman is expecting a child, her immune system naturally absorbs cells from her foetus. With some women, cells belonging to their baby can still be found in their skin years later. Billie had once read that somewhere, and she had liked the romanticism of the idea: bodies bound together for all time. But what about the father? In Billie's case, Uncle Henri – the uncle associated with presents, walks and summer sunshine – was all she needed.

It was that summer when she was thirteen. She had returned home well before nightfall, earlier than usual. They had been so wrapped up in their discussion that they hadn't heard her come in. Louise's forehead was furrowed, whether in anger or sadness it was hard to tell. She was staring strangely at Henri. Billie could not see the expression on his face, she could only see him from behind, leaning towards Louise. He was whispering.

I'm here, I see you both, Billie thought she heard.

You know nothing of our lives, Louise was saying.

Henri reached out his arm towards Louise's hand, but the hand withdrew, shrank away.

'Your letters! You think letters are enough? She's your daughter, for God's sake!'

Louise had straightened up, making her taller. Uncle Henri, meanwhile, was shrinking, rocking from left to right as if trying to dodge the flashes from Louise's eyes.

'I've forgotten so much, Henri. If I let you come, it's for her sake. As far as I'm concerned, I've forgotten you.'

Louise talked and talked endlessly. Billie had never heard her express herself with such force. She didn't know her mother was capable of such an outpouring of words. Uncle Henri was drowning in the flood. His back was hunched, he was casting about for a way out.

'Stop it, Louise! Don't say things like that. You don't really mean it.'

At this point Louise had slumped down. The change had been instantaneous, as if the spring holding her up had suddenly given way. She had let herself sink into his arms and he was back in full possession of his powers. He would not let her gain the upper hand again. He was stroking her now and repeating the same words that said it all.

'My Lulu, what am I supposed to do? It's too late. It's too late. I've got my own life back home, my own family.'

Billie would have liked to get out of there sooner – to make herself scarce, take to her heels – but her legs wouldn't move. The words had invaded her. She had a whole army marching through her head. *She's your daughter, for God's sake! Your daughter!* She had been reminded of the play she had been rehearsing at school with Lila and the others, the play they would be performing at the end of the year. What was going on here and now in her own house bore certain similarities. Except that she had misjudged the roles of the characters, and now that they had revealed their true selves and showed themselves in a new light, everything had changed. Yet they would still have to return to the script, recite their lines and carry on where they had left off, taking on board this new distribution of roles. At the same time it didn't come as much of a surprise to her. She wasn't born yesterday. Did they think she was stupid? She already knew about that. The stage was all set, they just needed the actors to say their lines, to spell it out for anyone slow on the uptake, the lazy general public who always needed to be spoon-fed!

In the end Billie had slipped up the stairs, run to her room and hidden under the bedclothes, trying to silence the voices clamouring in her head. Later she had stood staring at her face in the mirror, her swollen eyelids. She had sneaked into Louise's room, rifled through all her make-up and dabbed her face with cold water. She had carefully concealed the red blotches and the circles under her eyes, and had highlighted her lips with lipstick applied with such a heavy hand that it looked obscene, laid on thick, and had a crumbly texture in the corners of her mouth. She had liked turning herself into someone else, a Bill with attitude. A proper little ruffian. Then she had smiled at herself in the mirror, put on her trainers and a denim jacket and gone downstairs to where the others were.

On her way down, she hadn't been able to make out clearly what they were saying, but she had registered the lightness in their tone. This told her all she needed to know. The storm seemed to have passed, and the voices pinged back and forth in the living room over the two glasses and the half-empty bottle of wine. Louise was in good spirits, taking it easy now. Her moods, even the darkest ones, always melted away once she had a nice glass of something in her hand.

'Billie, you're back! Come and join us!'

'No, I'm not staying.'

Uncle Henri had peered at her make-up. He had turned away, but she knew that look in his eye, she had long been able to decode his expressions. She could read him like a book.

She hadn't recognised herself at first in the mirror by the front door. For a moment she had been surprised by the stranger staring back at her: a girl with skin that looked patchy because the make-up had not been applied evenly, and a vulgar mouth drawn across the middle of her plaster-coloured face.

Was the thick layer of make-up that evening her way of hiding her pain – an unbearable pain that had no way of expressing itself? Billie was invincible. She had never needed a father, or at least only vaguely, secretly, before she had learned to live her life without one.

She's your daughter, for God's sake! It was at that moment, when Louise uttered those words, that something had snapped – something at the very heart of her, her vital force, as it were. Billie had not seen it coming, yet at the same time, in a way, she knew. A part of her, deep inside, had always known. But in V everything lay under a veil of silence.

'Uncle Henri' came and went, like the storms that erupt out of the blue in that part of the world. That's the way it would always be. In summer his red hair would sway with the river currents, he would smile at Billie and take her little hand in his before disappearing beneath the cloudy surface.

He was part of the world of V, that place where people went about their lives in silence, bathed in light but hunched over their own shadows. Once Billie was old enough to escape from there, this fake father would disappear along with everything else. My father, for God's sake! All that would remain of that cry would be a certain detachment, a desire to remove herself from the world so it could no longer harm her.

She recalls that absent father. His inhibited movements. The taboo that shaped their relationship. Uncle Henri.

She realises then how much courage it must have taken for him to drive over to the house in V after the funeral. He could have left again after paying his final respects to Louise. Left again as he always did. Yet he came to see her, his little Bill. His daughter.

He had knocked, waited for her to open the door, and smiled at her. *My condolences, Billie.*

My condolences, for Louise, for us, for your childhood. That is what he came to say.

So it seems the days they spent together did count for something. Do they both deserve a second chance? It was so long ago. It would take infinite patience to retie the knot between yesterday's and today's worlds. Not right away. Tomorrow maybe.

If Billie were to let him exist again, if he were to come back into her life now that they have made contact again, he would bring everything else with him: the icy water, the creepy crawlies, the corpses. Everything would be exhumed.

7

Billie has a leisurely stretch, her limbs pop and click; she lets her feet slide to the side, describing giant arcs on the sheets.

She has slept. This is such a rare occurrence lately that it puts her in a good mood.

She carries on in this manner until Paul wakes up.

'You remind me of a cat,' he murmurs, turning to look at her with half-closed eyes. 'That's how cats stretch, isn't it?'

She ponders this for a moment, thinks about the greediness of cats, the way they often have two homes. Two lovers. Like Adele. Like Henri.

'You're the one who's the cat, Paul . . . You're the Cheshire Cat.'

'The Cheshire Cat?'

'The cat from *Alice in Wonderland*, who has Alice dancing to his tune.'

'You mean the nice striped cat?'

'No, the smooth-talking philosophical cat. The one that appears and disappears without warning.'

A mobile phone rings and keeps on ringing in another room. Paul eventually gets up.

'His smile always stays, remember? His grin floating in thin air. He's the chaperone, the guardian angel!' he says, before disappearing into the corridor.

She can hear the hum of Paul's voice in the living room. In a few moments he will hang up, come back into the bedroom, slip his clothes on and bend down to her. 'See you soon, baby!' And she will meekly return his kiss. Then, like Louise and Henri, she will sit around waiting for him to return. And for the first time it crosses her mind that maybe she deserves better than this.

She jumps to her feet, puts on her swimming costume under a dress, grabs a towel and her bag while he is still on the telephone. She sees his bare buttocks against the backdrop of the trees of Père Lachaise. She gives a cough.

'Where are you off to, Billie?'

'Going swimming!'

The door clicks shut. She just catches a glimpse of him, naked in the hall with his phone in his hand. His gorgeous smile frozen.

She needs to reconnect with life, right here, right now, in the midst of the damp lockers, the hairdryers on full, the banging of the changing room doors, the wet floor strewn with hairs and footprints.

In. Out.

Her brain enveloped by her own breathing. Her powerful breaths amplified under the swimming cap.

In-breath. Her muscular arms thrust forward and back in perfect rhythm. They pierce the water, straight as arrows, barely disturbing the surface.

Slow out-breath. Her legs straighten out, opening like a pair of compasses, every atom of her body in perfect harmony with the water. The weightlessness.

In-breath. Her arms lunge forward again, forming the prow of a boat.

Out-breath. Her body is dancing.

She pulls the rubber cap down over her ears more. She is alone: sounds become a kind of distant echo, as if she were in a cave. She grips one of the bars along the edge of the pool, makes scissor movements with her legs and thinks about Louise's pampered childhood with Adele and Jacques.

The words of the manager of Les Oliviers come back to her – Louise used to pray for the soldier – and become entwined in her mind with Henri's comments about the nightmares that plagued her every night.

Billie shivers, her legs pedalling faster under the water.

Where is Louise's real father? Where is the soldier? She is desperate to know, and at the same time she has the urge to hide herself away, the way animals do when a storm is in the offing.

She pushes off from the edge, her legs thrust out like two springs, and disappears in a shower of water, wanting only to flee, to swim to the point of exhaustion.

She stops at the end of the lane to get her breath back. Next to her, a swimmer turns around and sets off on her next length. Her fuchsia pink swimming cap moves away, gets up speed. Billie washes away the mist that has gathered on her goggles, then she in turn propels herself off from the wall.

Under the water, the flapping motion of the swimmer's feet leaves a trail of thousands of bubbles merrily colliding and bursting. Billie plunges into the fizzing wake. She immerses herself in it and follows where it leads, with no thought of where it is taking her, or the distance still to be covered before she reaches the far end.

21 June 1946

It is the beginning of summer already! I haven't written for weeks. What can I say? ~~I'd rather not~~

Jacques has given me a taste of happiness. At last! His tenderness, his laugh and his sense of humour, which has emerged now that he knows and trusts me, give me strength in the face of my husband's ~~crue~~ brutish violence.

What can I say? I confess (I pray every day) that I would be glad if the man who shares my bed were to disappear, sucked into the black chasm of his nightmares for good. I wish he would leave us in peace, me and my Louise. That he would cease tormenting us.

Go away my loved one, my hated one. Return to the trenches of your delusions. Hide yourself away there and don't come back.

2 July 1946

My God!

What has he done? What has he done? ~~I'd li~~

For the last few days the heat has driven us outdoors, Louise and me. When we return from our walks, I look ~~in horro~~ at the smoke rising from our chimney. A fire burning in July, no less! It's madness!

He shivers all day long. The cold in his heart seems to have permeated his entire body, chilling his very flesh. He has taken to lighting fires and huddling up in front of them like a ~~lit~~ young boy. He stays there for hours staring intently at the flames flickering in the hearth. It's almost as if he is trying to see ~~thi~~ ghosts in them. These are among the rare times when he grows calm.

But this morning, dear God! This morning I left Louise in her little chair while I went to fetch my sewing basket (I have a lot of ~~dres~~ orders on the go at the moment). We sit upstairs, it's cooler there . . .

No sooner had I walked out of the room than I heard a scream from Louise. Such a ~~drea~~ cry!

I came running back and saw him standing there with the poker in his hand. He gave me such a ~~shee~~ distraught look. Louise had got up from her chair and was screaming, her face purple, contorted with pain. I scooped her up in my arms and ran to the kitchen to pour cold water on the back of her neck. My God, her pretty white neck! I think if I had not had Louise in my arms, I would have killed him on the spot! I would have killed him! I would have killed him! ~~I~~

He did what I told him straight away and ran to fetch the doctor.

Alas there's not much that can be done. The doctor said she will have a nasty scar.

But I'll do what I can to ease the pain. I have cut a potato into slices and I'll apply them to her burn several times a day.

Oh, her neck was so pretty . . .

I hate him

I hate him

I hate him

~~I~~

8

Billie has alighted at Alexandre Dumas metro station and is walking along Boulevard de Charonne, laden with shopping bags. The streets seem wider than usual – frozen somehow, as if a clock has stopped somewhere. There's always a lull in Paris during August. The tourists are there, as on every other day of the year. They cluster around the entrance to Père Lachaise and wander along the paths in search of the graves of their idols or stroll aimlessly. But apart from the tourists there is nothing. Most of the shops have their shutters down. The horns and sirens have stopped making their usual racket. Normally, Billie also likes to stroll the streets during those empty weeks when the Parisians have deserted their city and headed to the coast, the beaches, the islands and the mountains. In V she used to look out for them, the pale-skinned tourists who came to get a tan and let their hair down somewhere where the climate was more conducive to having fun. She and Lila could hardly wait. The fine weather would arrive, the heat would soon become oppressive, and that meant that soon Henri and all the others would be there. The new faces.

Walking briskly along the boulevard, Billie notices the spiky patterns of the graffiti on the closed shop shutters. It crosses her mind that she could take inspiration from it, it has the same appearance of nervousness as her thinkers. They, too, are an outlet for an anger that has no other way of expressing itself. If she came to this place in the twilight hours to do some hasty sketches like those artists from the shadows, like Adele with her secret jottings, would her inspiration return? Would everything that is churning inside her finally emerge onto the canvas? Ever since she returned from V, her hand seems to be paralysed. She keeps discarding sketch after sketch and time is going by. They call her. They press her. They explain that the exhibition has to be finalised this autumn, that without all the works in place it's not really possible to plan the layout. Billie is aware of all that, of all the implications of her delivering late, but she has lost her magic touch, the fluidity that has characterised her work in the last few months. There is definitely something inside her, a faint music that is just audible, a moaning and swelling, but she cannot seem to draw it out. Nothing will come. Neither a face nor a body nor a landscape. And the thing keeps growing inside her.

The heat is stifling; the handles of her bags are slippery between her clammy fingers. She makes a beeline for the shade of the plane trees on the central reservation of the boulevard. Joggers brush past her. She is repulsed by the sight of the elongated patches of sweat on their backs, and can't help thinking they are mad to be out running in this heat. She used to do the same as a kid – she would run all the way to the river – but that was different. She was young and the air was pure. She is breathing heavily now, worn out from the weight of her overflowing shopping bags. She spots a bench, turns towards it, and suddenly someone slams into her.

Billie gives a cry and lets go of one of her bags. The contents spill out over the pavement. 'I'm sorry! Really sorry! Let me help you!' The man is most apologetic. She can smell his strong odour as he bends down to pick up the brushes, sketchbooks and tubes of paint scattered at their feet. He asks her if she is an artist. A painter? An art teacher, maybe? She does not reply, and hastily stuffs the items back in the bag. Her eyes dwell on the swollen vein in the man's neck, the sweat on his arms and face. He smiles at her, apologises again and suddenly she has the feeling that she knows him. Or rather that he knows her. That he knows her name, knows where she lives and who she hangs out with. Because of the way he is eyeing her, that familiarity. 'Go away!' Billie whispers the words before repeating them in a louder voice, until he hears her. He looks at her, taken aback at first. His expression changes, becomes aggressive. 'Hey! Calm down! I apologised, didn't I?

What's there to get upset about?' Then she shouts. 'Go away! Shove off!' And she sees him step back and set off again in the other direction, resuming his run, cursing her as a lunatic as he goes. And all at once she feels other eyes on her. Those of the tourists, the locals, the idle shopkeepers and passers-by. All these people who seem to know her. Who seem to recognise little Bill.

And suddenly the twentieth arrondissement seems no different from the place she left. Where everyone knows everything. Where nothing can really be buried.

10 July 1946

The idea came easily to us. It was an obvious solution, a natural response to the kind of life Louise and I now led: a life filled with fear and hatred. Actions are not always as simple as appearances might suggest. ~~I owed it to myself to~~ *A good mother has a duty to save her child, even from its father . . . just as God saved Isaac. I did not need to explain it to Jacques: for him as for me, it was* ~~the obv~~ *an act of love. So we made a deal with each other under the big pine tree as Louise was babbling on her bed of earth.*

You will wait for him on the street corner, late at night, when he comes back drunk from one of his night-time sprees, reeling and spewing ~~incoher~~ *grievances. He will have enough trouble walking and finding his way home; he won't notice you are there. You will strike him from behind with a stone or a stick. And we will carry him down to the river. His body will drift until morning. God knows how far it will travel. The next day I will say that he has not come home, but no one will be worried (including me), because as far as they are concerned he is nothing but a* ~~lous~~ *drunkard staggering around at night in search of his house, who has probably fallen asleep on a street corner. Later, when they find him, his body will have already started to decompose. He will have a head wound. They will think he keeled over and bumped his head and that he fell into the river, in no fit state to swim, his body numbed by the shock and the alcohol. They won't pursue it any further, especially in the current dark climate.* ~~Why go look~~

I returned home with my heart pounding, clutching Louise close to my chest. I scanned the faces of the people I passed. I greeted them hastily, looking for any sign of misgivings in their expressive eyes when they saw me. Fear is undermining my reasoning. Maybe someone heard us when we were talking beneath the big pine tree? Maybe he or she was hiding behind a tree and is reporting us to the police at this very moment? Maybe they will come and arrest us, this evening or tomorrow, before we have a chance to put our ghastly plan into action? Then I will be separated from Louise and her deranged father will have to take care of her. I ~~don~~ can't let that happen!

15 July 1946

I ~~kno~~ can sense it, I am certain of it now. The other villagers know what we are planning. I could see it in my neighbour's pointed stare. Her eyes definitely lingered on me for longer than usual when I returned home this evening. I could feel the weight of her gaze on my neck. As I slid my key into the lock I thought I might faint. As soon as I had closed the door behind me, I leant against the wall and it took me several minutes to get my breath back. My hands were shaking. I put Louise down in her cradle and went straight over to the cabinet in the living room where the ~~alco~~ liqueurs and brandy are kept. I took a swig straight from the bottle. The alcohol burned my throat – I felt like spitting it out, but soon felt a gentle drowsiness come over me . . . My thoughts are clearer now, my courage is returning. It is late. I have plenty of time to write as he won't be back until the first glimmer of dawn . . .

I can't stop going over today in my mind. I was talking nonsense. There was no one in the wood. Just the three of us. But what about you, my Louise, looking at me like that with your innocent gaze, did you understand? How will you ~~jud~~ look at me afterwards?

'Are you going to be long? We need to get going, the table's booked for eight o'clock!' says Paul outside the door of the bathroom, where Billie has barricaded herself.

She hurriedly gathers up the sheets of paper scattered over the floor at the foot of the bathtub, which she has been leaning against for hours, for centuries, engrossed in Adele's words.

She quickly sizes up the laundry basket. If there is one place where Paul will never go delving around, then that is it. Adele must have gone through a similar thought process when she was looking for a place to hide her diary. Louise too, a few years later. Are secrecy and paranoia passed down in one's genes? Now it is Billie who is stressing, her cheeks blazing.

'Everything okay, babe?'

'Yes! I'll just be a couple of minutes!'

She stuffs the envelope in the laundry basket, right at the bottom, under the pile of dirty clothes, tidies her hair, splashes her face with cold water, conceals the redness of her cheeks with foundation, outlines her yellow eyes with eyeliner to give them a lift. Those pages belong to a bygone age, they are ancient history. As far as the present is concerned, nothing has changed. *I'm here.* Billie tries to smile at herself in the mirror before opening the bathroom door.

'Shall we go?'

The crossed-out writing on paper so old it could disintegrate in your hands; the ink, grease and tear stains: her mind is still full of them. In her head she is still there, in that antiquated building where a drama is looming. It will have a tragic ending, she can feel it in her bones. She had been tempted to pretend she was suffering from a shocking headache or an attack of nausea and needed to return to the flat straight away, so that she could then delve down to the bottom of the laundry basket and immerse herself in the words again, re-read them to make sure she had properly understood.

Instead she is sitting at the back of the restaurant where they go from time to time – they always pick the same table, which is discreet, out of the way – opposite Paul, who is busy studying the menu.

'It was a nightmare this evening! It must have taken me an hour to get parked! It's crazy for August! Do you know what you're having, Billie? Shall I order some wine while you're looking?'

The waitress returns with a bottle of Chablis, opens it and pours a little into a glass, which she duly presents to Paul. She is so young. Her complexion is so clear. Fine, ash-coloured hair, accentuating the pallor of her skin. While Paul is tasting the wine, Billie observes her blue eyes, the way they protrude from her face. He puts down the glass, appears to be deliberating, weighing up the pros and cons, before delivering his judgement. This whole rigmarole he goes through . . . All of a sudden it strikes her as ridiculous.

'Perfect!'

The young waitress fills the other glass. Billie focuses on the sound of the wine being poured into the glass, but Adele's words are still going around in her head: *We will carry him down to the river. His body will drift until morning.*

'Are you ready to order?'

It's her pallid complexion that bothers Billie. Where has this girl come from, how did she come to be here, complete with her pale face and piping voice? Billie doesn't know what has caused the nausea to well up in her throat. But on second thoughts, she does. She knows perfectly well.

'We'll have the ribeye steak and the sea bass.'

She knows what those eyes remind her of, those bulging blue eyes round as marbles, the marbles they used to swap – Lila rummaging in the tartan bag where she kept her treasures. *I'll give you this one for three little ones! Look how beautiful it is!* It was an exquisite large marble with a kind of blue wisp visible, flame-like, inside the clear glass sphere. Billie had hesitated. She fingered the three marbles in her pocket, tempted by the blue flame. Yes, the big one was definitely worth three small ones. *Okay, we'll swap!* Lila's eyes lit up, she hastily plucked the three small terra-cotta marbles from Billie's hand and held out her precious one in return: *Here, Bill, it's yours!*

'The steak rare?'

Billie had examined the big marble, holding it right in front of her eyes to get a better view of the blue flame that appeared to lick the glass. She had felt an acute urge to touch that flame.

'Are you listening, Billie?'

Paul is addressing her. He takes her clammy hand in his.

'You all right, baby? You've gone all pale all of a sudden.'

The young waitress has come to light the candles in the variously coloured little glasses in the centre of the table. The flames cast dancing reflections on their faces. Sitting opposite Paul, Billie feels hot, so hot. She dares not turn towards the young woman to her right. No doubt she has a smile playing on her pale lips. Billie can imagine it – she doesn't need to look. She knows that two cute dimples appear when she smiles and that, if you lean close enough to her, you can make out the network of veins beneath her skin.

Billie sees the charmed expression on Paul's face. Her stomach contracts. *I'm here!* Under the table, she digs her fingers into the palm of her hand, harder and harder, so that the pain will bring her back to the here and now. She sits there with a vacuous smile on her lips, even though the sounds all around her are now drowned out by a humming that has invaded her brain. *I'm here!*

She looks directly into his blue eyes, plumbs their unfathomable depths. She thinks of the marble in Lila's little hand, of the flame dancing inside it.

'I need to ask you something.'

'Yes, baby?'

Paul leans towards her. His gaze seems so gentle now, warmed by the candlelight.

'How long d'you think I'm going to wait for you?'

'Sorry? What—'

His smile is still in place, even though he is squirming on his chair, ill at ease.

'How long? Come on, how many years, would you say . . . ?'

Behind Paul's silence, the deafening roar of the river wells forth from the restaurant basement, completely enveloping her. Above the tablecloth, her body pitches as if on a rolling sea. The water is going to engulf everything.

'Would you like desserts?'

Paul turns to the waitress, glad to be let off the hook for a moment. But Billie has finished her interrogation and falls silent. She closes her eyes because the pale body is right next to her once again. She has seen it elsewhere, that pallor. The pale body thrashing around in the water. It is that of her sister, her twin, her friend. Her dear friend. Her stomach is protesting loudly; she is wracked by terrible pangs.

'I . . . I'll be back,' she manages to murmur as she leaves the table.

She walks slowly at first, weighing every step. She closes her eyes for a moment, as if by shutting down her vision she could also halt the reedy voice nagging away in her head. *Wait for me, Bill!* She covers her ears, orders the voice to stop, to cease its racket. *Hey, Bill, help me!* She makes her way down into the restaurant basement, which has the feel of an overheated cavern. A tunnel taking her far away. Far back. To a time long gone. To the bank of a river, in scorching heat, to a little girl with an anaemic look about her, a twin who is a twin no longer. *Bill, help me breathe! Please!*

She reaches the sinks and her sleepwalk is over. Her hands grip the edge of the washbasin; a sick feeling rises up from deep down inside her. She lets it all out, along with her rage.

'What's going on, baby? I thought you were ill . . .'

Seeing her return, Paul has stood up, all of a sudden pressing her for answers.

'You want to know what's going on? Really?'

She looks as if she is thinking, but everything is crystal clear now.

'What's going on is that I . . . I really want a man I can call at any time.'

'But baby, you know you can always—'

'I want a table out on the terrace,' she interrupts, 'long holidays and breakfasts for two. I want to meet your family. I want to have shouting matches and proper reconciliations. I want shopping lists and cupboards too small for both of our belongings. I want to wake up next to someone. And I want you to want all that. And most of all I don't want to wait for you any more.'

'Calm down, Billie. We'll talk about it when you—'

'No! That's just it. We won't talk about it! These things, Paul, these things I want, they're acts of love. Simple acts that nurture our soul. You know what I mean? In the end, without these acts, we'll wither away. It's . . . It's like a mother and her baby. She nurtures it. And the same applies to ourselves: we can save ourselves, we have to.'

'What do you mean, save ourselves? You're not in your right mind today, Billie.'

'On the contrary, Paul . . . Things have never been clearer. It's all obvious to me now. You see, for a long time, I thought I deserved nothing better than that. Those little crumbs you fed me. I thought all the rest wasn't for me . . . That I had to stay cut off from that, always. But I do want those simple things, I want them a lot. And I think I'm entitled to them.'

'Are you leaving me, Billie?'

9

22 July 1946
We did it.
~~Last night we~~

Jacques and I have to be careful. We are going to avoid each other for the next few weeks until people's minds have stopped working overtime and the ~~spec~~ rumours have fizzled out. Meanwhile, even if it is risky – who knows whose malicious hands my diary could fall into – I need to write, to recount what we have done. These pages will be my sole place of confession, for no ear shall hear of my deed. I shall ask forgiveness of God, my father, my mother, my brothers – my dear brothers consumed by the war. These will be my last entries in this ~~terri~~ diary.

~~We~~

Where do I start?

I watch Louise running towards me. Her legs wobble still. She is learning. Her mouth makes bubbles of saliva, her arms swing through the air and I carry on singing.

> *As I was walking*
> *By the clear fountain*
> *I found the water so lovely*
> *I had to bathe*
>
> *. . .*

I think about his body in the river. How far has it ~~float~~ drifted?

I thank the heavens for the peace and quiet this day. Such light is rare, even in summer!

This day, 22 July, is a special day.

Louise is two today. It is her birthday.

It is the start of ~~her~~ a new life for her.
A life without bloodshed ~~or hat~~
My remorse is fading.

We did it.

We did it.

We did it.

Those appalling words. How can she carry on reading after that? First she needs some air. She is suffocating.

Billie crosses the living room, opens the windows wide, but there is not a breath of air. The night is warm, the air is oppressive. The outlines of the trees and vaults of Père Lachaise stand out in the darkness. She counts them. What else is there to do? Sleep won't come now, not with her head full of the soldier, Adele's lovers, the hatred.

Her eyes skim the paths of the cemetery, the inscriptions on the headstones. She doesn't need daylight, or to come closer, to read them. She knows them by heart. Her eye has often wandered over the inscriptions without her registering the magnitude of the words. *In loving memory. My beloved father. My daughter.* All those lives. Whole families buried along with their secrets. Their shame and their regrets hidden well away, carried with them to the grave. But those secrets speak louder than the tangible traces the living and the dead leave behind. They are passed from generation to generation in a look, a subconscious gesture, a silence. And each family member in turn reaps the repercussions. Just as a pebble striking the surface of the water sends out a series of ripples. How many of these descendants find themselves grappling with buried secrets, trying to put a name to the thing that haunts them?

Billie sighs, follows the line of the perimeter wall with her gaze. She peers through the darkness, trying to pick out the stone figure crouched over the two funeral wreaths she is holding firmly in her hands. Her head is bowed towards them beneath her veil. Who are they, those two departed souls she so cherishes?

The telephone rings again. It's Paul, pestering her. She switches off her mobile and disconnects the landline. Something more urgent awaits her. Her thoughts turn to the white walls of the Rue des Rosiers gallery. To this last portrait, the one that will round off her series of sombre thinkers.

She sits down at her work table, places the canvas in front of her – the impossible canvas she can't seem to finish – and fingers the charcoal. She waits for her hand to awaken. She wants to enter into a trance-like state where nothing exists besides the work that is taking shape. She scrutinises the vaguely defined face on the canvas, which has been appearing and disappearing for days. It can't seem to find its definitive form, its contours unravelling almost before she has drawn them. It is a face falling apart.

Gazing at these scraps of flesh, she is struck by a sense of trepidation, a feeling of dismay and abhorrence. Is he the one she has been trying to draw for days? The grandfather mutilated in combat? The soldier? The one whose face she has never seen, but who populated Louise's nightmares? She repeats Adele's words aloud: *Your shattered face . . . My beloved with the shattered face . . .*

And she flips. In a fury she rips the canvas to make the face disappear. That figure who haunted Adele and Louise, who seems to be menacing her now as well. And then she turns her fury on the others. For this is not the only face that repels her all of a sudden. The others do too. All of them. Her sombre – overly sombre – thinkers make her sick.

So she does it.
She does it.
She does it.
In the dead of night, she destroys the lot of them.

At daybreak, as the light steals into the living room, she surveys, exhausted, the canvases scattered all over the floor. This is more than a mess. What's happened here is a calamity. An emotional crisis that has sown mayhem, caused the festering abscesses to explode and brought the stagnant waters to the surface.

She sits down among the shredded canvases and surveys them for a moment: pensive faces, hysterical women, blurred expressions . . . Fragments of an austere, monochrome world that she has brought forth from herself, a dab at a time, while time stands still and only her hand moves. A birthing process.

She tries to sort through the canvases: perhaps some can be salvaged. But they are beyond repair. Did she really do that? Was it she herself, or the other one, the Bill from the river, in the oppressive heat, under the beating sun, the one who went swimming in a vile temper with a knot in her stomach, together with her twin who isn't her twin any more?

Billie fetches a Stanley knife and some large bin bags and finishes the job.

The village was shrouded in darkness. Everyone was sleeping. I am tempted to go so far as to say that death was on the prowl, but I must stick to the facts. Put everything down on paper, deliver myself of the burden ~~and bur~~

The village was slumbering, then . . . The few windows still lit at that hour cast their ~~feebl~~ light into the darkness. I was sitting on the ground, on the grass set back from the road. If anyone had passed that way they would not have been able to see me. But no one passed by, no one but the wandering cats that came to sniff at Louise, who was sleeping cradled in my arms. I had not wanted to leave her alone at home: it was out of the question. Imagine if he had arrived home earlier than usual by a different route. I do not know how long we stayed there, petrified . . . I was shaking uncontrollably now. Jacques was standing a little way off, on the street corner, waiting for ~~hi~~ our prey. From where I sat I would be able to hear the blow to his head and the sound of his body collapsing. I would go over to Jacques and together we would carry ~~the dea~~ the body over to the wheelbarrow hidden close by.

As I sat waiting, I recalled the terror in Jacques's eyes when we parted to go to our respective hiding places a few metres apart. He gripped my arm but then let it go. I thought he had changed his mind and wanted to tell me that it was folly, that we had to forget this evil plan. But I stepped back from him, I turned my head away – I knew that if I looked at him, I might back out and it was too late for that! We couldn't change our minds now. I am not ashamed to ~~sa~~ write that I was already obsessed with the idea of my new life. My deliverance was so close, I couldn't give up now. If Jacques did not succeed, I would do it myself. Yes, the thought crossed my mind, so determined was I to be rid of him once and for all. I was sure to find a way. There are easy ~~altern~~ methods like rat poison or other poison or smothering him in his drunken sleep . . . Plenty of people have done it and succeeded.

A noise made me jump. I sat up so abruptly that Louise woke up and started crying. I panicked. I desperately tried to quieten her so as not to attract the attention of the people in the houses closest to us, and meanwhile I thought I heard the sound of a struggle (though I could not be sure because of Louise's sobbing). There was a succession of blows, followed by the sound of footsteps. I couldn't see a thing, and my heart was hammering in my chest. Louise must have sensed that we were in danger because she started wailing even louder. I was ~~bes~~ frantic, and desperately clamped my hand over her mouth. I was so busy muffling the baby's cries that I was no longer paying attention to what was happening on the other side of the street. All of a sudden I heard rapid steps coming towards us. I looked up and shielded Louise with my arms ~~to prote~~. In the darkness I couldn't work out where the sounds were ~~coming from~~.

The shadow that appeared looming over us came out of nowhere. His hand grabbed me by the neck. I just had time to recognise the figure from my nightmares, the one I loathe above all others.

Oh God! My cry was soon cut short by the lack of oxygen. The vicious fingers tightened around my throat. I felt my head roll back, my body being drawn down towards the ground. Louise, clinging to my front, froze in astonishment. She was no longer crying. What baby can stop themselves crying like that? Oh God! As my breath dwindled, Louise, pressed against my body, started to become too heavy for me. At this point I realised that the man who had me trapped was enjoying himself. He could finally have his revenge on the world, on the war.

But the terrifying shadow crashed to the ground, his grasping hands releasing their grip. In the darkness, face to face, with the smell of his boozy breath in my nostrils, I saw his surprised expression. He stared at me as if noticing me for the first time, then slumped to the ground. I think that in that final split second he remembered who I was: not the woman living in fear of him, but the one who had waited by the side of the road long ago with a rose in her hand.

Jacques was standing over the limp body, close by. I, too, had fallen to the ground, exhausted by the struggle, by my efforts to breathe. I still could not catch my breath properly. He took Louise from me, and I heard him murmuring calming words to her. He was so gentle with her. He was injured, and had blood running down his forehead.

I think about my husband's savagery, about the risks we took. How could we have been foolish enough to believe that it would be that simple, that a blow to the head in the darkness would be enough? I was lying on the wet grass, where dew mingled with blood, with the stars above our heads, and Jacques was speaking to me. I was smiling at him but I didn't understand what he was saying. I could no longer hear a thing, not even Louise's crying.

It was no use. I was so tired, I was cold. I wanted to sleep. I wanted him to wake me at daybreak and place Louise in my arms.

PART FIVE

Three-Step Waltz

I

Before the cemetery gates were closed, I hid behind a vault and waited for night to fall. A starling came and pecked at the ground not far from me. I sat motionless, watching it go about its business, for so long that my legs went dead. At length it flew off. I looked up towards the tall chestnut trees and saw it had grown dark. I could no longer make out the ground. I groped my way along the cemetery wall and followed it, letting myself be guided by touch, like a blind person. It seemed a terribly long way and fear started to grip me. I heard a cracking sound to my left, which made me jump. A crow took flight, cawing as he went. It was at that moment that I spotted her, suddenly revealed by a shaft of moonlight falling between two branches. I approached and knelt down in front of her to get a close look at her face. But in the darkness, the stone veil completely hid it from view. Bending closer, I saw that the two funeral wreaths she was holding in her hands had been cleaned. I tried to decipher the names engraved in the stone. I scraped away the last traces of moss and finally the letters emerged. Bill. Lila. I howled with sorrow.

Billie is woken by her own cry. She pushes back the sodden sheets, feels for a dry place in the bed as her breathing settles.

She is wide awake now, but the sorrow is still there, that ache in her gut. This terrible sorrow that she has carried around for twenty years. It is as though Lila has taken up residence inside her.

And yet on reflection, after what she has read in her grandmother's diary, it seems to her that the sorrow was there well before. With Lila this sorrow, already latent in her, ballooned into something huge. Maybe Billie had always carried Adele, Jacques and the soldier inside her. Those monsters.

All of a sudden everything seems to make sense. It's all so very obvious and so very complex. It's like a cloth woven over time, the basic structure slowly evolving, yet still connected to its point of origin. First an initial horizontal thread sets out from a precise point, tightens, fastens itself somewhere. Then a second thread starts out from the first, and so on. The threads multiply and criss-cross until they have formed a complex weave. Some call it transgenerational memory, but for Billie it is a work of art.

Do monsters beget monsters? That's what Louise had asked Henri when she uncovered the scar hidden under her hair. That was probably what Louise wondered in the moment that she first set eyes on Billie, her own daughter. Bill, too, was the product of the same ghastly breeding ground. She can still feel Louise's gaze on her skin, that way she had of observing her, keeping her at arm's length. Billie, the fruit of her womb, who bore such a resemblance to Adele. That monster.

Louise didn't know how to love her daughter because she was inhabited by her secret and because she was probably terrified that a vein of violence might live on in her child. Was she wrong? Billie shudders as she thinks back to her last summer in V.

She imagines her mother finding the diary while sorting through Adele and Jacques's belongings after the accident. Discovering that her own life is based on a lie. Then reading the account of the crime, a cold-blooded, premeditated crime. How could she not curse them?

Louise removed every last trace of Adele and Jacques from the house. And removed every last trace of God as well.

Then she hid the diary away and, from that day on, became the guardian of the secret. The shame. She thought that burying the evidence would erase Adele's crime for good.

However, she had not bargained for the collateral damage. She hadn't realised that not only do the things you keep hidden live on, they actually gain in potency. Nothing can be erased. Billie knows that better than anyone.

Like the waters of the river, buried secrets find their way into even the tiniest spaces. They inhabit you and inhabit your children. They leak, return in a different form. Would Lila have happened had it not been for the soldier? Would Jean have happened? Would he have been able to turn their lives upside down in the way he did if there hadn't been a crack there already?

Billie thinks of the house in V overrun with spiders. Their elaborate webs adorning the walls and vibrating with the struggles of their captive prey.

How long do walls keep their memories? Where are the voices of those who once lived within them?

Should I have waited, lingered in the house before getting back on the road? Should I have worked through my memories, tried to weave them together so as to recreate the complex fabric and make sense of them?

Louise, you open the door and call me. You instruct me to go and pick some wild flowers in preparation for your man arriving. A ray of sunlight shines through the window and your face is back-lit, sparing me the sight of your chilly expression.

Adele, it is you who passes by like a draught of air, just behind me. You whom Louise both loves and abhors. You, whom she flees. You she wants to escape to when her daughter clings to her like a little animal. 'At least give me a hug before you go,' Billie cries to her mother, but she turns away, and those tiny hands become claws.

I'm thirsty. So thirsty.

Billie sits up and glances around the room for the bottle of water. She spots its reflection in the mirror opposite the bed. Seen from here, her back looks bent and twisted like a bit of old metal. It is as if she has aged overnight. She didn't know it was possible to age so quickly.

She would like it if, right next to her, where the sheets are cool, a hand were to reach out and touch her skin. She would like not to be alone any more. She takes a swig of water then lies back down.

Tick tock. Tick tock.

Time goes by unbearably slowly. She ought to get up, but her body refuses to budge. Outside, the sun has risen, a sliver of light slants in through a crack in the curtains, spotlighting her as if she were on trial.

Tick tock.

She quickly snuggles back down under the covers. Her head is inundated with images and there is nothing she can do about it. The hill is a beating heart. Water pumps out of it to a regular pulse. The bodies bob on the surface, swept along in the powerful flow. The blood leaves a pinkish trail in the water, which is washed away by the currents.

Tick tock. Tick tock.

The hill terraces slow the course of the water and create pools. Natural swimming pools. It is there that they used to bathe. Billie would watch the big mosquitoes hovering above the quivering surface of the river. She would stay perfectly still so as not to frighten them, then wait for the right moment and clap her hands together. The mosquitoes, taken by surprise, didn't have time to fly away. Having caught one, she would then crush it smartly between her thumb and index finger. *Splat.* And its abdomen would burst open.

Tick tock.

Lila's hair dances in the river, sparkling like an emerald, chilly like a cold room. Her unravelling blonde plaits are buoyed up by the underwater currents. The worn-out hair elastics have sunk to the bottom.

Tick tock.

She is so pale. White as a shroud. Shrunken. Curled in on herself. How long has she been like this? Years? Centuries? Everything is a muddle. The time for atonement is never-ending.

When did Billie wake up? Was it a few minutes ago or a few hours ago? A door banged somewhere in the building, and since then she no longer knows whether she is really here, whether time is passing in the normal way, or her day has vanished into thin air and it is already about to grow dark, whether she is simply drowning in the soft bulk of the mattress or in deeper currents. Where is she? Should she wait? Wait for the haunting echoes of the river to swallow her, or take matters into her own hands, finally take the plunge? Go and confront them.

Her telephone vibrates on the bedside table. She sticks an arm out and picks it up. 'Hello? Billie?' It takes her a few seconds to recognise the man's voice on the other end. 'I've got some good news.' She listens intently. 'A couple . . . I took them to view the house. They're very interested.' She has a sharp intake of breath. 'I'll come down!' He gently tries to dissuade her. 'No, no, there's no need for you to travel down. We can handle it remotely.' Billie sits upright. 'I'll come down!' She drags herself out of bed. 'I'll be there by the end of the day!'

The humming in her ears is back, the machine is starting up again. She decides to go by rail. She will take the first train, regardless of what it costs. It will take longer, but she can still be in V the same day.

She goes back into the bedroom, pulls out her travel bag from under the bed and starts packing – suddenly in a rush, as if her life depended on it. She gathers everything she will need for two days, three at most – her wash bag, underwear, two t-shirts, a skirt – rolls them into a ball and stuffs them in the bag.

She puts on a pair of jeans, some trainers, a jacket just in case – down south you have to be prepared for thunderstorms, which come and go at whim.

2

When she gets to the house in V, she swings back the shutters to let the sun in, and opens the windows to dispel the dust and the stuffy smell. She whips off the sheets covering the sofa and the other furniture. She takes in the worn fabrics, the yellow floral pattern on the armchair where she used to like to curl up, the scratched wood of the sideboard, the little side table. Looking at the light streaming into the living room, she wonders for a moment how she could manage to bring the house back to life. Not much of its contents remains, but the basic elements are still there: the building's original skeleton, its peculiarly shaped rooms, its upstairs shower room, its narrow corridors, its fireplace, the cracked floor tiles, the little balcony.

Then Billie goes up to Louise's bedroom and sits down on the bed. The old springs creak. She lies down for a moment, breathing in the smell of the clothes she has brought back from Les Oliviers. She runs her hand over the last dresses her mother owned, and finally the tears flow.

Now she spreads out the contents of the shoebox on the bed. She recognises the items – she has already held all of them at Les Oliviers. Her fingers have started trembling again. She no longer has any control over them; they are like nervous animals. Among the jumbled pile, she spots what she is looking for: Louise, standing in front of the oleander bush, her arm outstretched, her mouth a circle, a hint of amusement in her eyes, which seem to look at Billie from across the years. She turns the polaroid over to re-read the words on the back, the carefully written name. *With Suzie*. She recalls the person whom, aged nine, she used to call the 'fishnet woman' on account of the tights she wore in winter, remembers her gaudily painted lips planting greedy kisses on Lila's cheeks. 'Give her a bit of space, Suzie!' Billie and her friend – her sister – tear off towards the river, the father's appeals still hanging in the air. 'She can't be tied to your apron strings for ever, Suzanne! Let her live a bit!'

Had she targeted accusations at him in return, her overly lax, over-confident husband, after that dreadful summer? 'She needed keeping an eye on! She needed us! We should never have let her go off on her own!'

Billie re-reads the writing. *With Suzie.* She never tires of studying the fishnet woman next to Louise. Her striped swimming costume, her flamboyant lipstick, even on a day trip to the seaside, the shadows under her eyes.

She strokes the photo with her index finger. The Louise from those days in V has a sly look; she is smiling at the photographer with a slight air of disdain. Billie had almost forgotten that spark in her mother's eyes. The way she would come to life all of a sudden, shake off her stupor and demand to be the centre of attention.

'Is anyone there?'

Billie gives a start when she hears the voice downstairs.

'Yes, I'm upstairs. Just coming!'

She leaves the contents of the box higgledy-piggledy on the bed and hurries down the stairs.

'Hello, Billie. You made good time!'

She slows down at the sight of the couple walking towards her. She offers them a limp hand as the estate agent quickly runs through the introductions.

'We love it! We're completely enamoured, aren't we, darling?'

The two heads nod in tandem in her direction.

'We've already thought it all out, how we're going to organise the space. All we need to do is reconfigure the layout a bit and we could turn it into something a-maz-ing! Plus, you've got the loft: there's room to put in two children's rooms there. No, really, it's exactly what we're after! We're thrilled to bits! Aren't we, darling?'

The two of them nod again in perfect symmetry. The estate agent is over the moon. It's not every day he secures a sale this quickly. What couple in the prime of life would choose to come and hide themselves away in this hole?

'I suggest you come into the office and we'll go through—'

'Wait a minute!'

The three faces turn towards Billie.

'Do you have a light? I think I left my lighter in Paris,' she mutters, rummaging in her bag in search of the imaginary item, her heart pounding alarmingly in her chest.

'Sure. Here you are! Keep it. I've got another one.'

He laughs as he passes her the lighter.

'I need to tell you . . .'

She savours her first puff. Seldom has she been as sure of anything as she is of what she is about to say now.

'Yes?'

They stare at her.

'I'm sorry. I'm not selling any more.'

3

Lila and her parents lived on the high ground at the far end of the village in a very ornate-looking house that seemed to be in two distinct parts: upstairs were the cramped dormer bedrooms that they were planning on doing up one day, for the arrival of the little brother who would never materialise, and downstairs was the light-filled living room with its large bay window giving onto the garden. They had completely refurbished this room, Lila's father used to proudly tell everyone. They would do the rest at a later date, a room at a time.

Billie remembers going up this hill when she used to run to Lila's house. With her adult body, the route seems shorter to her today, but also more tiring. She stops half-way to get her breath back. It's probably her nerves that are making her breathless, that part of her that is reluctant to carry on up the hill and wants to go back. But she needs to carry on, she needs to hold her head high when Suzanne comes to the door, to meet Suzanne's gaze without flinching. To face up to her.

The front door opens directly onto the street. You have to go through the house to access the enclosed garden. Her fingers slip on the doorbell, so the ring is cut short. She prays no one is home now, in the middle of the afternoon. 'You shouldn't be staying cooped up on a nice day like this! Go on, out with you!' That's what Lila's father would have said. The chances are he said the same today and they have gone out somewhere. She jumps at the sound of the key being turned sharply in the lock.

The figure is standing back from the doorway, so all she can see is a silhouette. She can't make out the face in front of her. She could still change her mind, leave without a word. But in the dark hallway, the silhouette suddenly moves. 'Billie! Sweet Jesus, it's you, Billie!' Two hands clasp hold of her, wrap around her. 'What a surprise! My goodness, you've changed, Billie!' The eyes blink. Two gleaming marbles. 'Come in! Come in, don't be shy! You know the way!'

Billie is sitting, stiff and uneasy, on the sofa facing him. She has an uninterrupted view of the garden. It has been neglected; the weeds have gained the upper hand and she can see no sign of either the plum tree that used to grow against the fence or the clumps of lavender and rhododendron. She is disappointed by its size as well: back then it had seemed huge to her. It used to make a wonderful playground. She spots the shed at the bottom of the garden, a hotchpotch of old panels, which, by some miracle, is still standing. Their childhood realm.

On the dresser in the living room, just to her right, Lila is looking at her and smiling her big gappy smile. She has lost two milk teeth, the front ones, which gives her a remarkably mischievous look. She sports a fringe, and Billie searches her memory in vain; she has no recollection of that fringe. The photo must have been taken in late summer: the orangey light lends warmth to the little face, which has a scattering of freckles over the nose, brought out by the sun. She seems so alive behind the glass. She looks at Billie, almost as if she were about to jump out of the frame to come and talk to her.

'Suzie won't be long. Would you like some more lemonade, Billie?'

'Yes, thank you!'

He leans over carefully, his hand shaking slightly under the weight of the jug. He used to be so strong. She used to picture him as some kind of giant. Nothing could diminish him. He was a bull.

'You know, I don't want to disturb you, I can always come back another—'

'Billie! Please, you don't need to stand on ceremony! You were like a d—'

'May I use the toilet?'

She stands up; she really doesn't want to hear what's coming next.

'Yes, go ahead. You remember where it is, don't you? Just under the stairs.'

The wall of the narrow corridor leading to the kitchen and toilet is lined with masses of framed photographs. There were fewer in the old days. It is a veritable wall of remembrance. Lila is there before their eyes every day. Lila as a baby, a child, then a teenager, extraordinarily pale, roaring with laughter, with her hearty, unchanging laugh – on her own in most of the snapshots, but always leaning a little to one side, as if she were already making space for the little brother who never came.

In other photos Suzanne has an arm around her or is standing behind her. She looks into the lens with a half-smile, her chin resting on top of her daughter's head. Her expression is serene, contented. She looks gentler than Billie remembers, perhaps because of the absence of her loud voice and uproarious laughter. Billie especially remembers Suzanne's flamboyant laugh, her clichéd expressions, her habit of singing at the top of her voice in the house – *'Et si tu n'existais pas, dis-moi pourquoi j'existerais!'* – in front of a horrified Lila and Billie, who clapped their hands over their ears, and Lila yelling, 'Stop it, Mum! You're out of tune!'

'She was beautiful, our little Lila, wasn't she?'

Billie jumps; she had not heard her come in.

'Suzanne!'

'D'you remember how she wanted to be a ballet dancer . . . ?'

'No! Really? I'd forgotten that!'

As Billie ponders this snippet that she had consigned to oblivion, Suzanne leans towards her and kisses her.

'"I want to be a star," she used to say. We arranged for her to take lessons. She had the whole outfit, the tutu, the ballet slippers . . . but in the end, there was no getting around the fact that she wasn't supple enough. She kept on with it, though. She was determined, our Lila!'

They stand in the corridor for a little while peering at the photographs, Suzanne close enough to Billie that she can feel her body heat. Has she always worn that heady perfume?

'I was so afraid we'd forget, that she'd disappear all over again. But she's here with us, isn't she, Billie?'

Suzanne is looking fixedly at one photo; she seems to be miles away all of a sudden.

'I adored your mum, you know. I didn't know what to do when it happened. You were so far away. I managed to get hold of your Paris number. I wanted to let you know about the funeral, but I didn't know whether you—'

'I know.'

Billie recalls that day, back at her flat in Paris, when she had been terror-stricken at the sound of Suzanne's voice. It had come as a terrible shock. She had come a long way since then.

'Lulu was always a hoarder, as you know. She would never throw anything away. Literally, not a thing! It was as if she liked collecting useless junk. Even cinema tickets for films she'd enjoyed. I tried to gather together a few knick-knacks, old souvenirs . . . You wouldn't believe the clobber, Billie! I went to see her at Les Oliviers. We had a look at those old souvenirs together . . .'

'I'm sure Louise was pleased to see all those things.'

She places her hand on Suzanne's shoulder. She is surprised by how insubstantial it feels. She remembers it being more rounded.

Standing there in the corridor among the myriad photographs of Lila, Billie is surprised to find that she enjoys hearing the stories about her mother. For the first time in a long time, a certain sense of calm descends on her.

'Suzanne . . . That summer . . . That dreadful summer . . .'

'I know, Billie.'

'No, that's just it, you don't know! That day, I should have—'

'Stop it, Billie, I beg you. It's not your fault. It's no one's fault.'

'But I should have—'

'You were just a child, Bill! The two of you were just kids! Our precious little girls, so pretty . . . Lila and Bill. Bill and Lila. It's that love you have to remember, Billie. Nothing else. Through you, Lila lives on.'

She listens to Suzanne telling her stories – some mundane, some preposterous – stories that make her want to burst out laughing, like when they called her Bill and it made her fly into a rage. She goes back to gazing at the photos. She memorises the happy faces. Suzanne's chin propped on her daughter's head behind the glass frame. Then, further along, Lila astride a low wall, standing next to a swing, in front of a fairground merry-go-round, with candyfloss stuck to her chin, standing in the sunshine in her swimming costume, her sandals in her hand, one eye closed and an ear of wheat clamped between her lips, in a party dress with her face made up, or rigid in her winter coat . . . Billie relishes all these versions of Lila, those vivid details that made her unique – the bright sparkle in her eyes, her stubborn expression, the dimple in her left cheek, her freckles in mid-summer, her sickly pallor. She knows each of these features so well. They are part and parcel of her memories. She moves further down the corridor and her mantra, the one she has been reciting in her head all these years – *if one doesn't talk about a thing, it has never happened* – suddenly strikes her as a ludicrous mistake. Everything was here. Everything is here. Nothing is really forgotten. Further along she comes across one last snapshot: the pair of them, two slender figures hand in hand, wearing shorts and sandals, forgetting to look at the camera, about to dash off.

Can one ask the dead for forgiveness?

4

Just kids, Suzanne had insisted. Our precious little girls, so pretty. But what were they, in actual fact? They were neither children nor adults, but something in between. Young warriors roaming the hills, one in search of oxygen, the other love.

Beneath the broad leaves the air is humid, warm. The trees imprison her like a lid closing over her. Billie breathes in the smell of wet earth. She revels in it as she walks, avoiding the tangle of roots poking out of the ground. It seems further than it used to. At last she detects the sound of running water ahead.

Her stomach contracts. She runs. Then the river is there before her. The water transparent beneath the canopy of greenery. Its emerald hues, fractured in places, appear darker in the rocky hollows.

Billie stands still. The deafening noise engulfs her.

She surveys the unchanged landscape. Looks for the two little tearaways roaming the river bank. Looks for the two figures, both still lily-white as summer approaches. Listens for the echo of their laughter.

Balanced on a flat rock, she takes off her outer layers, leans closer to the water, dips her toes in to gauge the temperature. She shivers. How did they used to get in? On the water's surface, large mosquitoes perform their graceful dance.

She slips off her underwear, closes her eyes and dives in. In the icy water she struggles to breathe; she thrashes like a puppy. And yet they used to spend hours in here, goodness knows how. Little by little she relaxes, and swims for a while with small brisk strokes to warm herself up. Then she stretches out flat, her body floating perfectly horizontally, her belly button pointing out of the water towards the sun.

It feels so good . . .

They are there, close by, Adele and Louise. She feels them. Minute insects caught in a complex web, curled up like foetuses. They move their arms and legs, send vibrations along the threads that hold them. They are ready to leave their cocoon.

How can she extract their story, transform it into carefully chosen words? Perhaps, by speaking the unspeakable, she can neutralise the curse. This river, the scene of all that has happened, could become the receptacle of their story. The words that Billie chooses will continue to resonate here. They will exist here.

Adele. Louise. Bill. They uncurl from their foetal position and timidly unfold their bodies to inhabit their space.

'Let's start at the beginning,' Billie breathes, maintaining her position.

5

In the beginning was God.
Our Father, who art in heaven,
Hallowed be thy name,
Thy kingdom come,
Thy will be done on earth as it is in heaven.

Adele prays in silence, articulating each word in her head. She recites the prayer twice more to be sure of being heard.

She lies down on her front. The protruding mattress springs press into her thighs and her stomach. Her arms are wrapped around the pillow. Her breathing slows, free of all hindrances. Her mind runs free, her thoughts travelling to far-off places.

In the dead of night Adele waits for her god to comfort or reprimand her. To show her the way, with kindness. Always with kindness.

In the beginning was ecstasy.

Her lover's skin smells of musk. Louise breathes it in, sucking it down into her lungs. She wants to dress herself in this scent, envelop herself in it. It will be her perfume. Primal juice.

Beneath the skin of its abdomen, the rutting deer creates a treasure that is round as an orange. A gland containing the dark liquid, that brown secretion. Musk.

The libido mechanism is set in motion. The buck secretes the magic substance that will captivate the doe, drive her crazy.

Before the act of mating, there is the scent. This juice of wood, of earth, of flesh embodies sensual ecstasy.

Louise inhales the organic smell. She feeds on it.

In the beginning was the breach. The rift. A white-hot sword tearing the film, the skin.

The gates open, sweeping the fine membrane aside to make space. Inside, everything is in place, the way is clear.

Lips are parted into a scarlet flower. Its petals quiver as the living mass fearlessly eases its way between the smooth walls. Flesh moves on flesh, acquiring a fiery glow.

The release comes abruptly, without warning. It is a thrust towards the light. A battle.

First the head. Wet, purple, emerging from the depths.

The little body is catapulted out; it lands in rubbery, gloved hands. The ultrasound monitors are rendered redundant with the first furious, formidable cry.

The storm of spasms is over. Under the fluorescent lights, the world is metallic. Cold.

The gloved hands envelop the tiny body, warm it, clean it. They rub it gently, wipe away all that came with it. The blood, the mucus, the tears.

But beneath the flesh the roots remain. The gloved hands can do nothing about these roots; they are lodged in the depths of the womb. The uterus is a path from a region so remote . . . What will she have brought with her, this little girl with the cat's eyes, round and yellow like two gold coins? What will she take from her mother's milk? What will she reject? No one knows.

Their three noses are bent forward over their bowls of soup. 'Our Father, who art in heaven, we thank you for this meal . . .' says Adele's father. She bows her head, certain that her god is looking down upon her from above, that He sees into her and knows her innermost thoughts. She clears her mind and focuses on her father's words.

'God is love, he watches over us.'

Under the table, to her left, she catches sight of her brother, the younger one, crushing a bit of bread into a ball between his fingers and flicking it at the leg of her other brother, the older one, sitting opposite him. The younger one giggles. Adele is furious. Her brothers are blaspheming her god with their flippant behaviour. God is anger, she muses.

'Let's eat, children,' says their father.

The four spoons plunge into the soup. Slurping noises fill the dining room. Adele observes her brothers' faces out of the corner of her eye, their skin where spots and hairs are now sprouting. They eat up their soup, wolfing it down; their changing bodies need a steady supply of food to fortify them, make them strong.

God is anger, she repeats in her head, fingering her bread. They're going to pay for what they've done.

As her breath fills it out, the fine rubbery membrane stretches until it becomes a ball as big as her cheeks. It gives off a strawberry scent. Louise pops the bubble of gum between her teeth. She peels away the bits that stuck to her lips when the bubble burst, then takes the whole globule of gum out of her mouth and wraps it around her index finger, sucking on it contentedly as she leafs through her magazine.

'Louise! Dinner's ready, sweetie,' Adele's voice calls from downstairs.

'Okay, Mum, I'm coming.'

She allows herself one last page of *Vogue*: Brigitte Bardot, the flare of her skirt, the soft drape of the fabric, the pink and white pattern of the gingham . . . She keeps coming back to the skirt, its shape, the pattern on it. That's it, she resolves, that's what I'll ask Mum for for my sixteenth birthday. It is in six months; they will have time to go and choose the fabric and she will get her mother, with her clever fingers, to recreate that thing of wonder.

But most of all it is the narrowness of the waist that obsesses her. How does Bardot manage it? Louise slides her finger over the photo, tracing the line of Bardot's body from the waist to the hips, then she compares the outline with that of her own body. She feels the bulge just below her belt. She hates her annoying curves; she wishes she could be hollow. I need to eat smaller meals, I need to get Mum to stop feeding me up like a pig!

Her parents are growing impatient downstairs. She jumps off the bed and tears the page out of the magazine. This evening she will show her mother the twirling skirt she wants for her birthday.

The girl with the yellow-rimmed eyes has shot up like a weed. So quickly. Is she the product of her mother's womb, or of dry ground? The time of classrooms, of dressing up, of secrets never to be divulged – I swear on my mother's life! – of lifelong promises, of daring and of headlong races through the fields gives way to the time of silent escapades, of desire – that butterfly that takes flight within you – and of fear. The boys from the village start taking an interest in her. They watch her as she crosses the main square.

Billie walks slowly, concentrating on her hip movements. The wobble in her ankles when the tip of her sandals meets the soft ground is the only sign that might betray her nervousness. The material of her dress sticks to her damp thighs and she discreetly shifts her hips to unpeel it. She has gathered her hair into a high bun that exposes her neck and lets her skin breathe.

The young people of the village are there, revving their mopeds, clustered in small groups like bunches of grapes. They know each other as well as if they were brothers and sisters, but stronger bonds have formed between some of them. The twins are there. Her heart skips a beat as she passes in front of him. She feels his eyes on her.

It is Jean whom she prefers, Jean the cold one, Jean the serious one. Jean who stands there like a statue while his twin brother struts around the village streets, sticking his hand up girls' skirts, casting them aside one after the other as if they were no more than a piece of meat. Billie knows she will never be caught in his net because she prefers the other one, the one in the background, whom she observes unobtrusively when she is sitting near him.

And she knows that he is watching her too. She pretends to be interested in what Lila is saying, but she is looking at him, she sees him straining to hear.

Adele stands in the doorway, watching her brothers making their final preparations. She hears their father's words, the words that will accompany them on their way to war. They will carry these words with them, will hear them every day, draw strength from them.

She steps forward into the room to say her goodbyes. The older one hugs her to him, embraces her passionately. She can feel his stubble getting caught up in her hair. He is tall, his arms are sturdy. He will be a hero of this war, he will come back triumphant, she keeps telling herself, trying to absorb this thought as she would a fact. He makes no attempt to spare her feelings. He knows the significance of this goodbye.

As she approaches the younger one, she is confronted with his pride, which he wears like a shield. He has already set off for the battlefield, impatient to prove the courage that drives him, to put it to the test. His secret fears will be left at home with his sister and his father. Once there he will be a soldier. Only his eyes betray his terror.

Adele takes refuge in her room after they have gone and she prays. She thinks back to all the times when she has invoked God's wrath upon them. She regrets that now.

God is anger. If they do not come back, it will be her fault. All her fault.

'You look gorgeous, sweetie!' says her mother, clapping her hands.

Louise twirls around, making the gingham skirt fly out, and finds what she is looking for in her friends' eyes: envy. She runs over to give Adele a kiss.

'Thank you, Mum, you're the best! It's exactly what I was after! It's just like the one in the magazine!'

Then she flies into her father's arms. She likes to nestle against his powerful chest, rubbing her head against his shaggy beard.

Her soft-hearted father, so awkward beneath his tough shell . . . Occasionally he stammers, when the house is full, like today, for her sixteenth birthday celebration. She does not look like him. She sees more of herself in her mother's features, but she has inherited her thirst for affection from him. He is the one she likes to snuggle up to, so little against his stocky body.

The candles have been blown out and are lying half burnt on the edge of the plate. The cake has been eaten. The wrapping paper has been torn open, the gifts it contained laid out on the dining table. Streamers have been tossed in the air, and one is dangling from the standard lamp. Louise and her friends, scarlet-cheeked, are yelling at the tops of their voices.

'Shall we go, girls?' Louise bellows.

They file into the hall and disappear. Their voices fill the alley.

Leaning on the railing of the little balcony of her first-floor bedroom, Adele watches the girls go. Louise looks ravishing in the skirt she has made her for her birthday. The puffy underskirts make it flare out below her waist, emphasising its slenderness.

Adele goes back downstairs and contentedly surveys the havoc in the living room.

'Let's have a tidy-up!' she says cheerfully to Jacques.

It is the village festival this evening and all the young people are there. Billie is nervous. She fiddles with the belt of her dress. She rarely wears dresses like this – low-necked and cinched in at the waist – and feels ridiculous. But she has chosen the outfit for him. Tonight she will dance and she will feel his eyes resting on her body. He will pluck up the courage to speak to her at last, and in this one, perfect night everything around them – the smell of alcohol, the noisy motorbikes, the fear – will fade away.

Billie heads over towards her friends, who are standing a little way off, sipping shandy. She passes a group of boys and can't help hearing their sniggering and crude laughter as she brushes by. She hates all of them. Their presence, uncouth and intrusive, is robbing her of any intimacy she might have with him. She makes it, with flushed cheeks, to where her friends are, flops into

a chair and her friends greet her with enthusiastic kisses. They
are all there, excited to be at the most hotly anticipated event of
the summer: Fran, the redhead, who has brought out the green
in her eyes with a lick of eyeliner; Sonia, slightly gawky in her
stretchy dress; Marie, caked in make-up; and Lila, cheerful Lila,
whose blonde plaits quiver as she roars with laughter, before
summoning the girls for a dance.

She is in the middle of the dance floor. She whirls around,
with her skirt flying out and her thin plaits thrown back behind
her, and it is as if a halo of light surrounds her. All eyes are on
her. Billie envies her confidence. She watches her and feels her
first twinge of jealousy. She is the one who should be there in
the middle of the dance floor, but it's impossible because Lila is
taking up all the space.

So she stays there slumped in her chair, staring straight ahead
of her, ignoring her friends who are gesturing to her. She is
petrified at the thought of seeing Jean's gaze alighting on someone
other than her. On her twin.

After school Adele runs straight to the river bank, and her hunt
is fruitful. She holds the quivering abdomen between her fingers,
brings the pin close and smartly pierces it. The slender body
bends to the right and stays suspended in that position for a few
seconds before surrendering, letting go of all tension for good.
She positions the butterfly nice and straight so that it is parallel
with the other corpses in the wooden frame.

'They're God's creatures,' her father says. 'Leave them be.'

God is beauty. I am carrying out His divine will, Adele decides.

In summer, as soon as the first warm days arrive, she sets off
armed with her net and stalks them in the woods, on the flowers.
She likes the way their colours dance silently. As they flutter through
the air, she is already thinking of the place they will occupy alongside the others in the frame. She brings the net down sharply.

This display of shimmering wings is Adele's pride and joy. She
has chosen ones that contrast nicely. It is her work of art.

It was while butterfly-hunting that she stumbled across the

young soldier. He was lying down and she didn't see him at first because he was hidden by the tall grass. She gave a start when she noticed his boot sticking out. She was afraid to begin with because she was on her own – risky in those troubled times – and she didn't know who he was. Her gaze travelled over his uniform, and up to his youthful face. He was looking at her with a slightly mocking expression, an amused twinkle in his eye, and a blade of grass clamped in the corner of his mouth that he chewed on. He ran a hand through his dishevelled brown hair as he greeted her. And they talked.

It came just like that, out of the blue. There was no pain, no prior warning. Louise just felt the warm liquid between her thighs, forcing her to run and hide in the toilet. She sits there on the seat, her mind racing. *What do I do? What do people do?*

She waits for the rush of blood to stop then shifts her thighs apart and sees how, little by little, the blood is colouring the water in the toilet. The red cloud slowly spreads and a pungent smell wafts up between her knees from the foul water. She has never smelt anything like it before. It is unfamiliar to her. She was not expecting it. Is this the smell of a woman?

It's come, she thinks. *It's here.*

She has stuffed a tea towel inside her pants and is wearing a loose-fitting skirt that gives no hint of what is going on underneath. The blood mixes with the red and white checked pattern, the finger marks and grease spots. The material becomes a damp, odorous mass.

It is all hers. This erupting womb ready to open up like the wings of a butterfly. She is a chrysalis in the throes of metamorphosis.

Billie and Lila walk briskly. The heat has driven them outdoors and they are making for the river. They pass several holidaymakers accompanied by children singing at the tops of their voices. They follow the dirt track, which is lined with bushes on each side, and pick blackberries and wild strawberries as they go. Then the

path narrows and veers off into rough terrain, and they follow
it downhill, avoiding the roots protruding from the ground. The
burbling sound of the water grows ever clearer. Above their heads,
the tall trees obscure the sky. Their sweat cools in contact with
the surrounding air and they shiver.

'Slow down, Billie!' says Lila, who hasn't stopped talking since
they left the house. She has been confiding secrets. Talking and
walking at the same time is making her out of breath.

Lila talks about Jean's caresses, about her own awkwardness,
about the turmoil he sparks in her. He has caressed her, placed
his hands on her body. He has kissed her, and the hairs of his
fledgling beard pricked her chin. At first they tickled her and she
turned her face away.

If, at this point in her account, Lila had turned to face Billie
she would have seen flames in her eyes, flickering then blotting
everything out. But Lila is content with the silence. She doesn't
look at her, has no inkling that a volcano is stirring next to her.
She suspects nothing. And Billie lets Lila ramble on. She doesn't
want to hear any of it, yet she wants to know everything.

D'you want to know what he did to me, Billie?

Yes, I want to know. Everything.

Lila has betrayed her. Her twin, her soul sister, her dear friend
. . .

Between the branches initially hiding it from view, the river
finally appears. The reflections glinting off the water's surface
dazzle them completely, and Lila stops talking.

Her father's back is racked with spasms. Adele can see it rising
and falling almost rhythmically. Under his thick shirt, his shoulders
quake. She hears his sobbing. She understands that her brothers
will not be coming home, that the war has consumed them.

She alone knows the reason.

When she says her prayers this evening, it will be her brothers
she begs for forgiveness rather than her god.

Praying will make her next confession easier. Adele dreads that
moment, yet is impatient for it. She visits the priest regularly to

confess her sins. She tells him everything, in minute detail. He invites her to recite a prayer and grants her absolution. So in the days leading up to this encounter, she mentally prepares her list. She knows she must not forget anything, but she is not sure that she always knows exactly what constitutes a sin. Should she talk about the butterflies? Should she talk about her brothers, upon whom God has vented his wrath? Should she talk about the young soldier she met when she was butterfly-hunting? About what they did afterwards?

Adele clenches her fists as she steps into the confessional.

Yet when it is all over, when she has listed all her mistakes, making sure none is forgotten, and has received the blessing and the Eucharist, she feels as if a weight has been lifted from her. As she walks home along the village streets, she feels as though she is flying.

Her feet have left the ground. Her soul is cleansed. She knows that her god is watching her from on high, that this evening, when she says her prayers, He will answer them.

'Stop it, Louise! I'm practising!'

Louise gives a condescending sigh.

'What's the point of it all anyway?'

She looks out of the corner of her eye at her classmate whose attention is firmly focused on the keys of the typewriter. Her index finger hovers, hesitating, above the letters before depressing the key. *How slow she is,* Louise thinks to herself. *At this rate it's going to take her hours to write that stupid letter.*

She lies down on her back and stares at the ceiling. She breathes into her gum and watches the wet bubbles grow and then burst, one after the other.

Typing! What a joke!

Louise is beauty. She is grace, she is sparkle – she sees it in her parents' expressions. She has natural talent.

She will be Aphrodite.

She will be a star.

Louise already knows the effect she has on boys. She likes

their shining eyes, the way their nostrils flare, the trembling of
their breath, their excitement. She counts her admirers; she knows
she can have any one of them at her beck and call. But they
aren't good-looking enough, mysterious enough.

The one who really intrigues her strolls around the village on
his own. He must be an only child, like her. His parents are
renting the house with the green shutters. They have moved in
for the summer. They keep themselves to themselves. They all
have the white skin typical of northerners.

He has red hair. Is he good-looking? Louise is not sure. He is
certainly different. At first he doesn't seem to notice her. It is
that initial affront that makes her decide that he is the one.

Louise has made up her mind. He will be the one she sets her
sights on. Henri will be the challenge from the north.

Her clothes lie strewn over a flat rock. From her hiding place,
Billie can make out the circular yellow stains under the arms.
She can see, lying on top of the shabby dress, the metal fasteners
of the hair elastics that held her plaits in place. Her sandals, caked
in a brownish mixture of earth and water, lie further down the
bank.

Concealed behind one of the trees that line the river bank,
Billie secretly watches the still water and the bather lounging
around in it. Between the faint splashing sounds, she can hear a
slight wheezing in her breathing.

> *As I was walking*
> *By the clear fountain*
> *I found the water so lovely*
> *I . . .*

She has been there a while, blinded by the reflections off the water,
sweltering, still as a statue. She has lost track of time, but she must
have been waiting there a good hour. Sweat soaks her cotton dress,
seeps into every fold of her skin, trickles into her eyes and hinders
her view of the bather. She wipes her forehead and tries not to
think about how thirsty she is. She stays there, determined.

Lila had come to fetch her to go down to the river, but Billie hadn't responded. Instead she'd stayed lying on her bed until the hammering on the door stopped. Then she watched Lila out of the window as she walked away with her towel tucked under her arm. She waited a good ten minutes before following her: Lila's erratic breathing made her slower than Billie. As Billie walked through the village, there was silence all around. Not a single movement disturbed the stillness of the streets. It felt as though the village was asleep, or dead.

> *I found the water so lovely*
> *I had to bathe*

Eventually the bather leaves the scene and Billie watches Lila plaiting her wet hair, putting on her underwear and her crumpled dress. She disappears, and Billie waits a moment longer before creeping out of her hiding place and taking a dip herself to revive her inert body.

She draws circles in the water and flicks its smooth surface with her fingers to frighten the mosquitoes away. She catches one and crushes it between her thumb and index finger, listening to the grisly sound of its abdomen popping. She imagines that it is her own body she is crushing.

The young soldier took Adele's hand and led her in through the rickety doorway. *There is nothing here,* Adele thought. But no, the truth was that everything was here, but in a state of chaos. Nature had run riot here unhindered, and nothing could keep the weeds at bay.

Anyone standing even a few metres away would not have noticed their hideaway because the tumbledown walls were submerged beneath the wild vegetation. As time had gone by, the weeds and grasses had gradually spread and taken over. The old building, hidden but still standing, was resisting the assault.

When he undressed her, dust fell on her bare shoulders and tickled her skin. She thought of the butterflies in their wooden frame, of the powder from their wings which got on her fingers when she pierced their abdomens. The dust, the powder: both of them light as ashes.

The bodily act is an act of love, Adele reasoned, as she headed home, ready to brave the look on her father's face. The act of love is a birthing process, a dawning light. That's what she kept telling herself to prevent her punishing herself, to block out the bad thoughts that were weighing her down.

Those crumbling walls will retain the smell of our bodies. We are lovers in this undiscovered place. It has given birth to us. It has made us in its image, Adele declared.

Louise knows something is not right. There are signs. At first she was proud of her swelling breasts – she even flaunted them under Henri's nose. Then came the ghastly nausea. This cannot be happening! Louise has long had her body firmly under control. She knows it inside out. It can decide nothing without her say-so. Yet it seems that a deception has occurred, that her body has taken matters into its own hands. Without her consent, it has embarked on the painstaking process of creating a new being. This thing is growing inside her and has taken root without her permission. She has lost control, just for a moment, and immediately all the actors in this unknown play have surreptitiously assumed their roles.

Breathe in. Breathe out. Fear paralyses her. The thought of death is lurking.

No, it is too soon, her life has barely started; Louise is a girl in the flower of youth. She was too busy observing all the changes in her own body to ever imagine that another could come along and spoil it. It doesn't bear thinking about. She dreads to think of the disastrous impact it would have on her life – her charmed life as a famous actress and idol – and the way people in V would look at her, the stares, the whispered conversations.

She goes over and over everything in her head, paces around and counts the passing hours, the passing days. Summer is drawing to a close.

And Henri? What help is he to her now that it has happened? Does she love him or hate him? It's all his fault. She hates him.

In any case, it is too late, much too late, she has made her decision. It's her choice. He doesn't need to know. He just needs to go back to where he came from. To the other end of the country.

Jean is swimming in the river, bringing relief to his heat-stricken body, when he sees Lila coming towards him. It is clearly not the first time. She already knows the momentous scene by heart. She must have rehearsed it several times, like the school play. That is, no doubt, why she takes off her clothes and steps into the water so calmly. Fearlessly. Under the glare of the midday sun, her eyes are two shining slits beneath her tangled hair. Seen from here, her hair appears white.

And she smiles. Two childish dimples appear on her cheeks as she approaches him. Their bodies intertwine in the cool water, under a heavy sky.

> *I've loved you for so long*
> *I will never forget you*

From her hiding place behind the leaves, Billie can imagine their saliva mingling into one, and the very thought of it cuts like a knife. She digs her fingernails into the palms of her hands until they bleed. *I'm here!* The cry is tearing her brain apart, growing there like a monster until its delicate walls explode.

Which hurts more? Having lost Lila or having lost Jean?

She is mesmerised, incapable of tearing herself away from the extraordinary sight of Lila and Jean together. From where she crouches, she can only hate them. This hatred is all she has. She hates this evidence of their beauty. The river signals their glittering triumph and its own capitulation.

> *Sing nightingale sing*
> *You of the joyous heart*
> *Your heart is made for laughing*
> *Mine can only cry*

She would like to crush them.

★ ★ ★

As the priest reads, Adele laps up the words.

'And they came to the place which God had told him of; and Abraham built an altar there, and laid the wood in order, and bound Isaac his son, and laid him on the altar upon the wood. And Abraham stretched forth his hand, and took the knife to slay his son.'

Adele's heart is beating violently in her chest. She prays for Isaac, the child of flesh, the innocent.

The priest continues with his terrible story.

'And the angel of the Lord called unto him out of heaven, and said, "Abraham, Abraham": and he said, "Here am I." And He said, "Lay not thine hand upon the lad, neither do thou any thing unto him: for now I know that thou fearest God, seeing thou hast not withheld thy son, thine only son from me."'

In Adele's eyes, Abraham's deed is a betrayal. It cannot be an act of love. To want to sacrifice the flesh of his own flesh is an act of folly. The demand that God makes of Abraham is pure vanity.

God can be cruel; that is the only lesson she draws from Isaac's narrow escape. From that day on, she becomes aware of the real possibility of a hell from which one must save oneself through a life of mercy. She must try harder. From now on she will always recite her prayers three times so as never to be punished by the hand of God.

And above all, she will obey the angel's words, to the letter: *Lay not thine hand upon the lad, neither do thou any thing unto him.*

Louise is naked and cowering behind the screen.

On this September morning she has made her decision and come to the address on the slip of paper the woman has given her.

Are you ready?

Yes, I'm coming. She does not recognise her own voice.

Look, here I stand before you. I am offering you my disloyal body. But wait, I may yet flee from here. A word from you could release me from this pit of torment.

'Are you sure of your decision, Louise? You can take more time to think it over, you know.'

Sorry? What's that voice in my head saying? I can't hear it. It's not getting through to me. Everything inside me is confused. I have become that little skinny girl again. Fearful, crouching in the dark, calling for her mother. Mother. What an appalling word. I will be a non-mother.

Yes, lady. I want to walk out of this room, but I lie down on your table. I am so cold. Look at my skin, all the hairs standing on end like fortifications.

The sun is shining outside. I can see it between the creased curtains. Its warm rays caress me, travel up along my spread-out legs. Their golden filaments twine around my ankles and my wrists. I barely feel them, they are so light. They raise my left arm, then my right. They straighten out my legs, first one, then the other. I am their puppet. They take me, deliver me. Today is not a day for mourning, they whisper.

Wait! I know you've got a job to do but I'd rather put it off until tomorrow. I've paid you anyway. So I doubt it makes any difference to you. Those needles, this table . . . I need a bit of time to think, okay?

I want to go down to the river to wash.

Tomorrow I will come back and see you. Tomorrow you will set an angel free.

They quickly undress, fling their clothes down on some stones. Billie stares at the two hair elastics. Now, from close up, she can see the strands of blonde hair snagged in them, yanked out accidentally by Lila in her haste, clinging to the fabric of the dress.

They swim for a long time, side by side, basking in the silky coolness of the river. As before, they have fun poking their heads into the cavity under the rocky ledge while the waterfall pummels their necks. They shout and listen to the echoes bouncing off the walls that encase them like a protective womb. Lila shouts the louder.

Billie finds her voice faltering. Her throat has nothing left to expel; she is empty inside.

'Hey, Billie, d'you want to know what he did to me?'

Lila's words feel like a thousand leeches. They fill her, then suck her dry, literally. Billie has never felt so empty; it is as though she has eaten nothing for days.

But Lila keeps going: she swims and talks and her breathing grows faster, more ragged. She is getting out of breath. Billie thinks to herself that at least that might eventually make her stop talking.

'Hey, Billie . . .'

She has long been familiar with the first signs of an asthma attack, the whistling that subtly infiltrates the breathing before the wheezing starts. Gross. It sneaks up stealthily. If Billie were not listening out, it would go unnoticed. How many times has she dragged Lila towards the steep rocks, made her lie down and helped her use her asthma inhaler. It is always reassuring for Lila to have Billie nearby. She knows someone is looking out for her, and so she tends to do whatever she pleases. She should know better, because Billie will not always be there.

The whistling is still faint, barely there. Billie lets herself be lulled by the sound of Lila's breathing, which is becoming more rapid.

'Hey, Billie . . . Billie . . .'

She listens to the rasping sound in her windpipe, a murmur that, strangely, seems to chant her name. It could almost be a song.

'Jean—'

Billie tilts her head back until her ears are fully under water. Then all she can hear is the dull rumble of the river as it collides with the rocks in its path. She screws up her eyes just enough to let a little light in without it dazzling her.

'Hey Billie, d'you want to know what . . .'

Enough! Who cares about the rest of the story! Who cares about the repercussions. She doesn't want to listen any more to these words that torment her. If only Lila would shut up. She doesn't want to hear her any more. Ever. She swims towards the river bank as quickly as she can. She has to battle the currents. All she wants now is for that loathsome voice to disappear, drowned out by the deafening roar of the river.

'Billie! Where are you going?'

She springs like a grasshopper from rock to rock. She grabs her clothes, doesn't stop to put them on. She is escaping. All she knows is she won't be coming back there any more. There will be no more Lila, no more Jean, no more bodies betraying her. Not ever.

'Billie! Bill! Wait for me!'

The disfigured soldier has gone, carried away by the river currents. His body bobs along on the water's surface until it strikes a sharp rock and a flap of his shirt becomes hitched on it. The body stays trapped there, in the same place, swaying left and right to the rhythm of the water like a deranged dancer. The slow disintegration of the flesh begins in the water. The skin will continue to decompose until the body is found by some unfortunate passer-by.

Adele murmurs a song in Louise's ear as she sleeps.

> *As I was walking*
> *By the clear fountain . . .*

High in the sky above their happy home, the sun hangs like a huge sunflower with its colours inverted: fire forms a glowing ring around its white heart.

Will the two of them stay rooted there, hypnotised by its light, like Clytie?

Clytie, the water nymph who is in love with the sun god, Helios, and spends hours admiring his dazzling beauty, while he continues on his arc across the sky, loftily ignoring her.

Lovestruck Clytie, who stays put and never gives up, until finally she is transformed into a sunflower, her head forever tilted towards the sun.

Does Clytie's agony actually end at the moment of her metamorphosis, or is it merely perpetuated in the form of a never-ending wait?

Will I stay forever riveted to the spot like Clytie, paralysed by the horror of what I've done? Adele wonders.

When will I escape from this living hell and walk with my head held high again?

'Louise, we are together,' Adele tells her daughter, and the sun blazes with a thousand fires, dazzling her and making her blink.

All is love, even our base, reprehensible actions, Adele keeps telling herself, as the soldier's corpse bobs on the water's surface.

'Lay not thine hand upon the lad, neither do thou any thing unto him,' the angel said.

She has obeyed the angel's command.

The river water is green and murky. It is Lethe, the source of oblivion. The water's surface has a silvery sheen in the moonlight. Louise goes there after dark. She takes off her clothes, feels the little bump in her belly. Henri has gone. She ordered him to leave, because of this thing growing inside her. She is nineteen and nothing will ever be the same again.

No, she is mistaken. She is still tiny. She is one year old. Tomorrow is her birthday, when she will be two. She cannot swim. She can barely even walk.

No, that's not it. Tomorrow she will be fifty-six and Henri has come back. She couldn't get him to stay. She never could. She crouches down to cup the water of the Lethe in her hands. She takes little sips of it and slides a little further into forgetfulness.

As she leans out over the river, she doesn't immediately notice the shadows gathering around her. Lila, her blonde plaits bobbing in the darkness. The soldier with his ravaged face. He bends down, smiles, and enfolds Louise in his arms. The hundred-year-old Louise. The baby Louise. Tomorrow is her birthday.

It is nearly the end of her first full year spent with both Adele and the soldier in the house with the low ceilings. Tomorrow she will be two. Her father cradles her in his arms, carries her into the water. In the light of the moon, the soldier regains his pre-war face. Louise grasps her father's curly hair in her little hand. She toys with it. The soldier's embrace is wonderful. He swims like a god. She nestles in the strong arms of this man who has the same blood flowing in his veins as she does. They traverse the currents together. He carries her towards the far bank, where the blonde plaits are bobbing.

One. Two. Three.

Three cottages rise out of the earth. A river runs between them.

The water is ultramarine blue verging on green.

It is here that the lifeless arm floats. The little curled-up hand on the end of it is various shades of cyan and titanium white. The face is bluish with hints of purple. The cold flesh is reminiscent of lilac petals . . .

What did Lila look like when they pulled her body from the water? Were there telltale signs of the battle she had fought? How did it happen? What is there to tell of Lila's end? Did her face contort, her mouth opening and closing like a fish's while her arms thrashed about in the water? How long did she stay afloat? Did she surrender quickly or did she refuse outright to accept what was happening to her? Heroic Lila waging her battle . . . Ensnared by the river, what kind of a fighter had she been?

Had she carried on calling Billie when she was already far away? But most importantly, had she had time to forgive her before succumbing to the murky water?

6

The air above the river has thickened. It has a peculiar density to it, containing what seems to be a trace of oppression. The silence is similar to the kind of silence you get in the eye of a hurricane; it hovers weightlessly above Billie's motionless body as the cold penetrates deeper into her.

One day she had collected a few belongings together and left V. How long was that after Lila's disappearance? Weeks? Months? She had been drifting aimlessly, starved of oxygen. She would head out of the village, walk for hours to escape Louise's dreadful silence, the poignant smile of Lila's father, whom she passed in the street sometimes – that bull of a man, broken. And in her head she could still hear the echoes of Suzanne's cries, which had filled the valley for days.

So she set off with her savings in her pocket, carrying nothing but a single rucksack filled to the brim. She had stolen away like a thief.

She can see herself light years back, the Bill of twenty years ago, leaving V with her head held high and her stomach tensed. Barely seventeen years old, a dopey look on her face. Wilting in the heat, she leans on her rucksack and drowses as she waits for the bus that will take her to the railway station. There are already indents in her shoulders from the straps of her rucksack. Yet the walk from the house in V to the bus stop only took her about twenty minutes. It is the same walk she used to do every morning on her way to school, her clammy hand in Lila's, from the time their world began. Sitting on the ground, she feels the wind's caress – the lightest of touches. It travels from her ankle up towards her calf, lingers in one spot, circles around on her skin in hesitant comings and goings. She opens her eyes and sees the tiny legs moving over her skin, retreating, zigzagging, climbing back up again. The ant perseveres. Billie waits for it to arrive at the summit of her knee; she watches it going around a beauty spot. She brings her index finger close, tenses it against her thumb and aims at the tiny creature. The finger releases like a spring, and the ant is flicked away, sails briefly through the scorching air and crash-lands a little way off.

Billie lights a cigarette and takes a long, slow first drag. She wants to savour it. With her face turned towards the sun, which is resplendent on this momentous day, with her loose hair tickling her shoulders and all her savings in her pocket, she feels so strong all of a sudden. And free. Terribly free. To the extent that it makes her dizzy. The late afternoon sun floods her whole being. The sky is orange-coloured; it bathes the hills in such a warm light that at one point her stomach clenches and she almost regrets leaving it all behind. The feeling only lasts for a brief moment. Once she is on the bus, that will be the end, the final full stop. Lila and all the rest, Jean, the river – everything will disappear the moment they round the first bend. Everything that has been done will stay hidden away here in the shadow of the hills. Deeds are fleeting moments destined to pass away. Matter is destined to pass away. Just a few miles and everything will vanish as if by magic. Whoosh! There will be nothing left behind but dust. In the end, it is so easy to leave, to take a different path. It is just a matter of leaving things where they are, the way they are. Turning away and setting off in a new direction. No, it is not running away. Billie's departure is not an escape. It is an impulse.

The bus has drawn to a halt in front of her feet with a hideous squealing. It opens its creaking doors. She mounts the four steps, takes her ticket, flings her bag on the floor and flops down on the back seat. She turns her face to the window, soaking up the light. And it is then that she cries.

Being young, she will have plenty of time to forget. Forgetting is a natural process; it shrouds things in a kind of mist, it surrounds

them in an aura, blurs the detail and makes them fly away, disappear for ever, in the same way the wind blows leaves, dust, ashes
into the air and carries them right out of sight, to beyond the
visible horizons.

Everything is dust.

She really had thought she would forget. But all she had done
was numb the pain for a while, and then the memories had
started haunting her again. She knew . . . Yes, she knew, or she
should have known. She knew Lila's breathing inside out, it was
part of her world. But she had blithely ignored the warning signs
that she was drowning. She had picked up her clothes and left.
Just like that . . . She had let her friend struggle alone in the
river. What did that make her? A coward? An imbecile? A monster?

She had cursed Jean, that troublemaker who had turned up,
awakened desires, opened up a can of worms. It was he who had
turned her into a monster. Or perhaps she already was one.

She had tried to forgive herself, to ease her burden of guilt:
after all, someone could easily have been walking by and come
to Lila's aid, dragged her over to a flat rock, laid her down and
waited for her breath to settle. That's what she had kept telling
herself, that ultimately it was down to bad luck. Negligence is
the only thing they could have accused her of, the furious citizens
of V, the bereaved, despairing at the loss of one of their own
children, at one in their grief, ceaselessly seeking to understand
how such a thing could have come about.

But Billie, as her friend, her twin, the one who went everywhere
with her, how was she supposed to carry on living after what
had happened? She would be the prisoner of her own mind, at
the mercy of the violent recriminations in her head that ebbed
and flowed like the tides. *Mea maxima culpa.* My most grievous
fault.

Beyond forgiveness: that's what she was until she found the
diary. In discovering what Adele had done, Billie also found the
source of the evil. An unimagined, oppressive evil that nourished
them with its sap. She needs to eradicate this evil: dig down to
its depths, pull it out by the root and cleanse the wounds.

She swims, shivering, to the first flat rock, where she has left her belongings. Her fingers are purple and rigid with the cold. There are two things she still needs to do. She leans against the rock and hoists herself up to reach her bag. Her shaking hands take hold of the diary, the letters. She clamps them against her front, swims off still clutching them, returns to the icy currents. Despite the cold, she concentrates on what she is doing. She tears out the pages a few at a time and throws them in front of her, watching them float for a moment before being immersed in the river. The water gently erases the ink, war, hatred, crimes of love. It dissolves the disjointed writing, washes it away. The currents take hold of the pages, sweep them along towards the lower reaches of the river. Billie watches them slip between the rocks, escape to a far-off place beyond the horizon.

Once it is all done she swims back to the bank. Her teeth are chattering, and she is shivering uncontrollably. She thinks of Lila's ordeal and summons up her courage. She hoists herself up on the rock. Its edge feels warm against her blue skin. She grabs her bag and delves her hand inside it. But she is in too much of a hurry: she cuts herself on the sharp blade. What an idiot! A drop of blood wells up on her finger. She sucks it away before grasping the knife. She resumes her jerky swim, returning to the same place where she is buffeted by the icy currents. She stays on the spot, treading water to keep her on the surface. When she brings the blade towards her neck, it dazzles her for a moment. She places it against the nape of her neck with the sharp edge facing outwards. She closes her eyes, tries to control the shaking in her arm. A flick of the wrist and the knife slices cleanly into the brown mass. The hair falls in clumps, scattering over the surface of the water. It floats for a moment before becoming sodden and sinking to the bottom, long black eels heading for a place unknown.

Can you ask forgiveness of the dead? Feeling the wave of warmth flooding her chest, she concludes that you can.

The ripples fade, and calm returns to the surface. Only the silent, peaceful dance of the big water mosquitoes carries on.

Epilogue

When she reaches Rue des Rosier, Billie pauses for a moment, glancing through the lit-up window at the crowd and the canvases on display along the gallery walls. It's already busy. The private view could turn out to be a success. Shivering, she turns up the collar of her coat. Behind the glass someone is staring at her. That smile . . . She blushes despite the biting cold. He has sent her so many messages over the last few months. Why was it only after she had left him that he had decided to fight for her? Although if he had done it sooner, she probably would have run away. She thinks about Henri and Louise's first meeting in the thunderstorm in V, about their shaky yet unfailing love, about that last unfortunate encounter at Les Oliviers. She thinks about how we think we have a choice, how we put things off until tomorrow, how we believe we have power over time, but that one day the unthinkable dawns on us: there is no going back.

So she smiles back at him, gives a little wave and goes inside.

'Paul! You've come!'

'I wouldn't have missed it for the world! Your new show . . . It's really lovely, Billie.'

'Thank you.'

'All those colours . . . It's not what I was expecting! It's so different from what you normally do. It's . . . How shall I put it? Hungrier. More alive. And what about your thinkers, Billie? What have you done with them?'

'Let's say I've moved on from them . . .'

Billie smiles. She casts an eye around the room, the walls plastered with acrylic paintings on canvas. It's a riot of colours. And smells. Just like V.

Blonde plaits swaying on a child's neck, voluptuous bathers on the water's edge, hundred-year-old walls with fault lines running across them, feet kicking up fountains of water, undulating countryside and sun-kissed blackberries, little figures running along dirt tracks, a pensive girl with tousled hair and a cigarette in her hand . . .

The story slowly takes shape on the canvases. The narrative strands fall into place.

Anyone viewing the paintings can easily drift from one to the next, suspecting nothing. Their eye discovers the verdant spaces, which they find delightful. They haven't yet noticed the crawling insects that have crept into the scene – the dead wasps and the inert bodies floating on the water. The way death is lurking.

Then there is the swimmer floating on his back, his face turned towards the sun. All of a sudden the brushstrokes are crude. The paintbrush has damaged the flesh. No, it is the face itself that is crude. Monstrous even. Disfigured. The giant with the deformed head floats, fully dressed. His clothes sow seeds of doubt. He shouldn't be there. He is out of place. A weeping willow on the riverbank arches over him. Its trailing branches are mourners. They reach out towards the motionless giant, dip their tips in the water, in the red cloud surrounding the head that is spreading in the water like menstrual blood.

One is tempted to turn away from the painting, take a deep breath and let one's eye seek other pastures.

Then the river is there again, its surface calm. The trees form a green canopy over the water. The sun filters through the foliage, speckling the canvas with masses of little golden dots. The eye takes in the whole before returning to the centre of the scene. Here it stops, unable to tear itself away from this thing it is witnessing. It takes in the hand reaching out across the water's surface, the youthful chest thrust upwards as if wanting to embrace the sky, the frightened eyes and the mouth gaping in the middle of the face like a crevasse. The little girl is looking at the sun and crying. No, she is shouting. Calling. She is not alone under the canopy of greenery. There is a shape in the background.

One doesn't notice it at first, its outlines merge into its surroundings. It is a long trailing branch. No, it is a person with their back to the river. A slim silhouette with an impressive mane of hair, she is moving away, slightly disdainful. Indifferent to the drama that is unfolding.

Beyond that are yet more paintings, more bodies, elated or luxuriating.

'Your hair, Billie . . . It's quite a transformation, but it suits you. You're—'

'Thank you, Paul.'

She blushes, instinctively places her hand on the nape of her neck. She hasn't yet got used to this contact with people, this kind of exposure.

'Tell me, where does the name of the exhibition come from? Why *V*? What does it mean? Is it someone's initial? Is it one of these women?'

'It's a place. An imaginary place . . . Or rather, it's a place that exists somewhere. A birthplace . . . Yes, that's it, it's a birthplace.'

'Where have you been all this time, Billie? I've been looking for you for months and—'

'I've been painting . . . and I've been gardening.'

'You've been gardening?'

'I've been tackling the weeds, digging them out roots and all. Such incredibly long roots they had. They'd invaded everything. You should have seen how deep they went, Paul, how tough they were . . .'

She starts at the sight of a solitary figure standing outside. The man shuffles on the spot for a moment, seems to be waiting for something. The tip of his cigarette draws little glowing arcs in the darkness. He throws away the butt, pauses, and finally enters the gallery. He unwinds his scarf, nervously, while his eyes travel from painting to painting. Billie could swear he's shaking. She sees him make his way towards one of the pictures, the one in which two little girls are running along a dirt track, hand in hand, their pale faces tilted towards the sun. They are moving so fast that their sandals are sending up clouds of dust behind them. The man leans towards the canvas to get a better view, and under the spotlight, his red hair takes on a fiery glow, like in V in the old days, when the light made his rippling hair shimmer under the water.

Before going over to join him, she takes a deep breath, casts her eye over the exhibition as a whole, the sparkling colours exploding on the walls – all those paintings that she has produced over the last few months in the house with the low ceilings. Her handiwork. The secret work of the women of V finally exhumed. Dragged out into the open. Offered up for judgement.

Opening the windows wide, letting in the light and the murmuring sound of the water, rediscovering the parched hills, reconnecting with the world of yesteryear: that's what she had tried to do as the summer slowly drew to a close and the tourists left in their people carriers.

Here, now, within these walls, V feels so alive.

Everything is here. Everything exists.

This book was created by
Hodder & Stoughton

Founded in 1868 by two young men who saw that the rise in literacy would break cultural barriers, the Hodder story is one of visionary publishing and globe-trotting talent-spotting, campaigning journalism and popular understanding, men of influence and pioneering women.

For over 150 years, we have been publishing household names and undiscovered gems, and today we continue to give our readers books that sweep you away or leave you looking at the world with new eyes.

Follow us on our adventures in books . . .
🐦 @HodderBooks 📘 /HodderBooks 📷 @HodderBooks

HODDER &
STOUGHTON